ONE MAN'S THOUGHTS

To,

Sita

with gratitude
and best wishes

Conway Dunn

ONE MAN'S THOUGHTS

Conway Dunn

ATHENA PRESS
LONDON

First published 2008 by
ATHENA PRESS
Queen's House, 2 Holly Road
Twickenham TW1 4EG
United Kingdom

Printed for Athena Press

With gratitude to Agatha, Cara and Gordon

NOTE ON THE TEXT:

The author's use of 'he' in the essays is not intended to exclude 'she'. 'He/she' is accurate, but seems cumbersome. Unless it is obvious that only one sex is meant, both apply.

CONTENTS

THE INDIVIDUAL

I start with the individual, with me and with you. Clearly I am a person. I have a life. In a quite literal sense it is my life, uniquely mine – it cannot be anybody else's; take it away and I am dead, existing only as decomposing material; then 'I' becomes 'he' and 'he' becomes 'his body', useless, to me.

No one has a stronger claim than I do to my own life. No one can possess it more closely than me, and no one can be as affected by its loss as me. Without it I am nothing, while every living being remains something. Naturally, it matters more to me than to anyone else. It belongs – in the sense of attachment – more to me than to anyone else. So far as my existence is concerned, I am my life.

Values grow out of facts. We see that we are fundamentally the same. This suggests equality, not only in fact – one species – but also in conduct; our treatment of each other. It is rational to deal with things that are the same as being the same, and not different. We have a sense of fairness. It is wrong to recognise equality, and then to practice inequality. Our conclusion is: treat one another the same. So we expect. So rights emerge. A right to life: we are as entitled to live as anyone else. A right to decide how we will live: we are more entitled to determine our own lives than anyone else. So we should be able to do as we wish – providing we do not infringe upon the rights of others. With this proviso, we should not be coerced into any opinion, belief, action or situation. Options can be presented, but we should make the choice, and others accept it.

What, however, if our choices clash? What if someone does not respect someone else's justifiable expectations? To avoid conflict, people accept law. Everyone gives up some freedom of choice in return for freedom from harm. Social rules, enforced by the police, provide security. Anyone who breaks the rules loses some of his rights, such as his liberty, even his life. The armed forces protect citizens from external threat.

Today we are born into such a system, and compelled to be a part of it, unless we can find anywhere on earth which is not organised similarly. Perhaps few of us want to try to opt out. We recognise the benefits of an ordered society; we agree that obeying laws and contributing to public services is likely to lead to a safer and a better life all-round, socially as well as practically.

So our freedoms are restricted, voluntarily. Bearing in mind, however, the starting point, and the ideal, freedom, and that our lives are ours, the restrictions should be as few as necessary, and to retain as much autonomy as possible people themselves should decide what is necessary.

Not always able to do as he wishes, the individual can, none-theless, say what he wishes to be done, and try to gain approval for it. He can cast his vote. Since there are different opinions, the nearest we can come to satisfying everyone is to satisfy most, so the vote of the majority of like-minded people should pass legislation, and the individual should comply accordingly – providing a law does not encroach upon his personal rights, such as to life, liberty, peace and possessions.

As far as is possible within society, each of us should be free to control his own existence. Providing the rights of others are observed, each of us should be able to do as he likes. I have my life. You have your life. I end with the individual.

MORALITY

Morality is concerned with right and wrong behaviour. It is not 'right' and 'wrong' in a strictly factual sense. Hence we use the word 'should' not 'is'. Morality is based on a mixture of facts and feelings processed into values.

One value most of us have is to preserve our own life. We strive to look after ourselves. At first, hopefully, we are assisted. Generally we are born into a family, which provides nurture and protection, and as we grow we realise that we are part of a more detached kind of family called society, which also provides protection, but, as well, imposes restrictions.

I do not want to be attacked; neither do others. So, assuming the principle of equality, society says no one should attack anyone. A law is passed: no violence.

Again, we have possessions and we don't want them to be stolen. Another law is passed: no theft.

These are the fundamental rules.

We are never asked if we agree with them or given the choice to disregard them if we don't. We are told from earliest times that they are right; to break them is wrong. In the past they were described as God-given, but there is no need to appeal to God; their inherent sense is clear enough.

The wish to preserve ourselves runs deeply, and one way of trying to achieve it is to make ourselves as strong as possible, in every respect. There are also the driving forces of ambition, materialism, status and fame. Of course, success can be gained within the system, but there may be opportunities and inclinations to achieve it by breaking the social code.

Then there are those who are disadvantaged or fail, and are in a poor, perhaps desperate, situation. They too may be inclined to break society's rules, for self-preservation or a degree of respite from misery.

In both cases the law-breakers may, in general, accept and observe social values, but they regard their own egoistical values as more important. It is a matter of priorities. They themselves come first.

Society, though, cannot tolerate such selfish behaviour, for if it did it would remove a major reason for its existence, and another reason, social interaction, would be threatened if one member could harm, or steal from, another with impunity. It is likely that individuals would retreat into their own homes and convert them into castles. In effect, there would be no society.

So offenders are punished – assuming they are responsible for their actions. There is a view that no one is responsible for any action: we are, as it were, complex robots acting according to, for example, our chemical composition.

Now most of us show that we can be aware of a situation and its consequences; we make a decision, supported by some reasonable explanation, and we are open to reflection and persuasion and, sometimes, we change our minds. Our make-up allows for these processes. I maintain, in another essay, that we do have free will.

If there is compulsive criminality, it can be treated as an illness, like any form of mental abnormality. In practice, the treatment might be little different from the punishment, for in each case the criminal would need to be restrained in some way and commonly this is in the form of confinement.

Moreover, even if we were, basically, robots, society could not just excuse and ignore all offences – saying they are wrong, but we can't help it – for if it did there may as well be no law; once again individuals would man their barricades and society would collapse.

Regarding circumstances as important, though, some people emphasise re-education rather than punishment. It is possible to combine the two: an offender can be compelled to attend re-education classes or courses. But will that alone suffice? A murderer could be reformed in one lesson. Assuming he really had changed would we consider that was sufficient? Some transgressors would merely pretend to have reformed.

Where a person is virtually driven into crime, that should be taken into account; where a person drives himself, he should be called to account.

So I turn to punishment. It means, essentially, harming somebody because they have harmed. It can be seen in terms of debt: a criminal owes society for the wrong he has committed against it and his punishment is a way of repaying the debt. There is the aim, also, that it will deter him and others from all crime. Debts differ in amounts and punishments differ in severity, according to the offence.

People are more important than property so, in principle, assaults are more serious than thefts and are punished more, though bearing in mind, too, degree and circumstances, a major theft may receive a greater sentence than a minor assault.

Another reason for grading punishments is that if there was only one for all offences, a criminal might be tempted to commit a more damaging crime since he would suffer no more for it than for a lesser one.

If a debt has been incurred, it is only just that it should be repaid.

Justice is commonly symbolised by a pair of scales; when the weights are horizontal they are balanced, and justice is all about balance, equal weight, matching; in short, fifty–fifty. That is fair!

Yet, where crime is concerned, justice requires more than a simple repayment of what was taken; more than, for example, repaying £10 with £10. It is not a straightforward business transaction.

Crime causes inconvenience and distress. There is the cost of investigating the act and holding a trial. The sentence needs to include retribution and deterrence. These factors have to be built into the fifty–fifty.

In many cases, of course, the crime is not one of theft, or only of theft, so even the initial repayment cannot be exact. The simple and just solution is to meet like with like, plus more to include the factors mentioned. So, perhaps, two eyes for an eye; two teeth for a tooth!

However, the leaders – the people themselves have never been asked – have rejected corporal punishment as brutal and, as such, uncivilised. Their response to serious crime is imprisonment.

Today, courts confine a man to a prison cell for years, occasionally for the remainder of his life, and within prison there is the possibility of further deprivation, including solitary confinement. This could cripple not the body, but the mind.

Though it would be just, I do not advocate doing to the criminal exactly what he did to the victim, and more besides, for that could involve demanding that those who are to carry out the sentence act in a way they may find repugnant and horrific, and in a way society does not want anyone to act. I maintain, however, there remains a place for some controlled physical punishment, such as a beating with some implement.

To the claim that such action encourages imitation, I think people can differentiate between the state's power and their own. We do not find citizens imprisoning each other or, until recently, hanging each other, because the state does it.

The difference between what the state and the citizen can do also applies to the objection that corporal punishment condones violence. Such a sentence would be imposed by a court, after a fair trial, restricted to certain situations and carried out in a measured manner.

The presence and use of military force does not condone war, but it is held that there are circumstances where it is better to fight than not to fight. There are situations where it is better to beat than not to beat a criminal.

To the view that violence should only be used as a defence to an attack, I can only uphold the claims of justice, deterrence and effectiveness. Justice demands a fitting repayment. Physical retribution would be another weapon in the arsenal of deterrents and, it seems to me, some potential criminals would be more afraid of a beating than of a prison sentence, which does not confront them with naked pain. A lengthy period of time is difficult to appreciate, and imprisonment itself can be taken more as a great inconvenience than an experience of suffering.

But I swim against the tide. Encapsulating direct bodily punishment within the very definition of brutal, the modern mood is to turn to fines, community service, threats of and actual imprisonment.

For justice's sake, sentences have to be matched to the crimes, but in most cases the sentences imposed are different to the crimes and so become a matter of opinion, and vary according to personal judgement, popular sentiment, the prevalence of a particular offence and, in the case of fines, to rising income.

A careless misdemeanour is at the lowest end of crime, and murder at the highest. Generally, if a crime is serious, the criminal is imprisoned – the greater the offence, the longer the time spent in prison.

Imprisonment, though hardly ever matching the nature of the crime itself, has become a common and the ultimate punishment. It can be seen as humane, and it is effective in the undeniable sense that so long as the offender is inside he is not outside committing more crime within society. The punishment lies, basically, in deprivation of liberty, choice and pleasures.

The disadvantages are that prison does not appear to be much of a deterrent. It is costly, and it can be wasteful, with many hours passing which are of no benefit to prisoners or society. Living with other criminals, a prisoner may be drawn deeper into crime. His family may find it difficult to cope without him.

Since crime involves expense – such as the loss of property or earnings, and the cost of the investigation and legal proceedings – at least part of the sentence should be monetary repayment. Retribution and deterrence may be met by a further financial imposition. If the criminal does not possess enough to pay the demand, he should be compelled to work, and an amount regularly deducted from his income until he has paid.

Community service is fitting where the community in general has suffered, for example, with vandalism. It would also be a meaningful punishment for a criminal who could shrug off a fine, especially if it was clear to all that compulsory – if not hard – labour was what he was doing. Public disgrace is itself a punishment.

For the reasons mentioned, prison should be a last resort, not automatically levied for 'serious' crimes, but to try and prompt an uncooperative offender to fulfil his sentence – if he will not work in prison he at least suffers its deprivations. Prison could also be used to contain criminals who are recidivists and those who have committed the unique crime of taking a human life. Murder is the deliberate killing of a person by another. The murderer cannot compensate the victim. The only just solution is to lose his own life. But executions, like beatings, are widely seen as uncivilised.

There is the possibility that an innocent man may be executed and if so he cannot, of course, be revived. We may conclude, therefore, that only where the evidence is blatant should the guilty be executed, and by blatant I mean beyond probability.

Modern society, however, has come up with an ingenious response to murder – life imprisonment. The guilty loses his life in a sense, but not a literal sense. He is deprived of much of what makes his life worthwhile.

But life imprisonment rarely means what it says. Distinctions are drawn between murders. Fundamentally this is unjust. The underlying principle should be one life for one life. Yet what should be done with the man who has killed more than once? He should be punished more. Given that there is no physical punishment, the only extra penalty seems to be harsher conditions within prison, such as providing only the bare necessities. This too, though, may seem inhumane, so the modem policy is to release some murderers – albeit under licence – before others, taking into account not only the number of murders committed, but also whether there was a history of discord, whether sadism was involved, and, of course, how likely it is that the killer will kill again. There is some justice in this, since those who have killed more, or more brutally, are indeed punished more.

War is another situation involving the deliberate taking of human life. The combatants aim to kill each other, and many do die. There are pacifists – those who oppose killing other humans under any circumstances – and probably their outlook will be respected. Members of the armed forces have, of course, committed themselves to fight if ordered.

The civilian non-pacifist, however, may be faced by his government, which should be protecting him, urging him to place himself in extreme danger; indeed, threatening punishment if he does not. It may well appeal to his patriotism, and it is likely that to a greater or lesser extent he is patriotic. He does not wish to appear cowardly. He may be convinced that the enemy really should be opposed. So he will answer the call to arms.

On the other hand, he may think that this particular war should not be fought at all. He may prefer to surrender than to die. Probably, his life is his most important possession.

As a member of society he has played his part. To demand that he should be prepared to lose his life for it is to turn society's fundamental purpose – protection – on its head.

If a government doubts that it can protect its citizens – in this case because its enemies are so powerful – the underlying contract is broken. Then it is for the individual to decide his response. Some people may prefer to stand and fight; some may prefer to be conquered than endanger their lives. Each person should have the choice.

It is the individual's choice, also, if he himself prefers to die than to live. Naturally the situation does not often arise. I think especially of euthanasia. A person may have a terminal illness, know that he will die in the near future, and to save himself pain, indignity and the loss of what he enjoys, he may prefer to die now. It would be a reasonable decision, and providing society is satisfied that it is indeed his decision and that he is not being coerced, then it should have no further say in the matter, assuming that the means by which the person intends to end his life are themselves lawful.

More difficult, because it seems more wasteful, would be the case of someone who is not dying, but who would still rather die. He may have weighed up his lot and found it a very miserable one, with no prospect of improvement, but rather deterioration. We might look for a better future, and urge him to consider it. Eventually, though, the decision is his. It is his life, and he who will be harmed. Others may be saddened, but he has priority over his own life.

Adding yet another dimension, a person may be healthy physically, but mentally ill – a chronic depressive perhaps – and want to die. Since he is ill – not in a normal state of mind – society may intervene, assuming that if he was not ill he would want to live. But if he cannot be treated effectively, he is somewhat akin to the first two cases, not terminally ill, but without a cure, and enduring a chronically unhappy existence. We could try to compel him to live in the hope that one day a cure may be found. But hope does not outweigh actual, unremitting misery. He is ill, yet we, who are not, can see that peace in death is a rational alternative to torment in life. Eventually, also, he should be allowed to die if he wishes, and if there is no real prospect of improvement.

Time is a crucial factor. We can all be hit by bad news, and our immediate thoughts can be despondent. Then, as our emotions settle, time passes and we think more, the outlook may not appear so bleak. So, before taking a fatal and final step, there should be a prolonged pause. The outcome, though, should be decided by the individual since it is a personal, not a social matter.

Society may advise, implore, regret, but it should not stop a person who has concluded he wants to end his life, nor should it stop anyone who is prepared to assist him. It is their choice and they who are really affected.

In the event, anyone intent on suicide, unless he is helpless, will succeed, with or without us, or social approval.

Abortion presents its own particular problem: whether or not to end an emerging life. An extreme situation would be a choice between the life of the mother or the life of the unborn child. I would give priority to the mother on the basis that she is already in the world, whereas the child is not. It would be an application of 'what you don't know, you don't miss'. I appreciate, however, the view that she has had a share of life; it is only fair that the baby should have a share too – in which case, I wonder if any distinction should be made between mothers of very different ages. Should, say, a fifteen-year-old be treated the same as a forty-year-old? One solution would be to follow the wishes of the mother herself.

I would also accept the mother's decision if she had been raped and become pregnant. What happened was no choice of hers, and to proceed as normal would be a lifelong reminder of the event itself. The child may even look like the father.

If a woman, for whatever reason, became suicidal about her pregnancy, and remained so, that too would be an acceptable reason for abortion. However, there would need to be as extreme a case as suicide, and this clearly and strongly indicated, for abortion means the taking of a life and this should only be done in the most exceptional circumstances. It is not justified by the prospect of some material hardship, or some distress, or that a child would be inconvenient.

In general, the aim should be for a birth, and in many societies welfare, including financial, assistance is on hand.

An issue that has arisen recently, not of life and death but of type of life, is 'designer babies': that is, by genetic treatment giving children particular characteristics. It is widely accepted that such treatment is permissible to correct a deficiency, but to use it to make a normal child more than normal in some respect is contentious.

It may be objected that this procedure interferes with nature. Nature, however, is not a purposeful force, but the world as we find it, without our adaptations; and we are, in fact, perpetually adapting it, not just to cure, but also to enhance. The aim here is to improve personal characteristics in the hope that the person will have a better life. Good, at least for the individual concerned!

Assuming that genetic enhancement would be expensive, those likely to make most use of it would be the rich, so they would gain another advantage and one that could continue for many generations. Yet there are always those who have more than others, and providing their money has been earned or won legitimately, it is theirs to spend as they wish, legitimately.

With their prowess, 'designed' people could benefit society as a whole. I can imagine a nightmare situation where these people become so dominant that they threaten the rest of us, but not for a while – if ever. At present the benefits are not so harmful to others that they should not be permitted. Rather, it is the subject of the treatment that needs protection, against risky experimentation, and against parents who may want features which the child itself, in time, may not want. There needs to be a protector of the unborn.

I have touched on some issues concerning life. To sustain it, we need food; depending on the climate, most of us need shelter. We protect ourselves with clothes, and a home – 'a roof over our heads' – and we buy items to use and enjoy in the home, to make our lives comfortable. These things belong to us; to take them without our permission is to steal them.

It is not a matter of morality that one person should possess more than another, assuming their possessions have been gained morally. I find it extremely distasteful that some people live extravagantly while others starve to death, and I would appeal to the rich to consider the poor, but to take away their riches is to steal them.

The government itself takes some of our money without our permission in the form of taxation. However, like society itself, the justification is that we want to be protected and looked after, and those who perform the work need to be paid, and the facilities and equipment paid for.

Administrators should be ever mindful, though, that it is our money, to be used for us, and we should be consulted about general allocations and major projects. It should not be wasted on luxuries.

Given that we are all entitled to the same service provided by the state – protection from harm, care when in need – we should all pay the same amount of tax. Income tax, therefore, is unjust. On this matter though, I confess my sense of justice is outweighed by my satisfaction that the rich are compelled to contribute more to the benefit of all.

Usually, we enter life within a family, and often, when we have matured, we start a new family. This is natural and useful. Traditionally the new family begins with marriage, which is a legally binding relationship, and so one partner can gain legal redress if the other one breaks his or her vows.

Clearly, many marriages do not last for life; vows are broken, differences emerge and if, despite attempts to overcome them, they remain irreconcilable, it is better for the couple to part, in divorce, than continue in unhappiness.

Recognising possible breakdown, it might seem sensible not to pronounce marriage as lifelong, but this would weaken the ideal. Divorce is a tragedy to be avoided, if doing so does not cause greater misery. Starting with the expectation that marriage is to last for life encourages more effort to mend rifts. The success of many marriages shows the goal is attainable.

Couples living together, but not marrying, avoid the ties, but also miss the protection of marriage, and so they should pay particular attention to the consequences of parting, especially if they have children. It would seem wise to draw up their own contracts.

Once upon a time, a man and a woman co-habiting without marrying was considered shameful, and unfair on their children, who were bastards. Once, also, homosexual unions were condemned as unnatural and abhorrent. Both relationships are now acceptable. Indeed, people are reprimanded if they do disapprove.

So I come to the shifting sands of public taste. Society may lean one way and the other, with smiles and frowns, but it should only prohibit when an action goes beyond dislike to becoming, at the least, a real, personal nuisance. If the act does not infringe on our lives, let it be. It is a matter of individual choice. One's own affair!

Custom, more than harm, is the prime reason for not permitting behaviour such as walking the streets naked, or having sexual intercourse or masturbating or excreting in public. In the case of excretion, hygiene, mess and smell are of course to be considered and they are also factors concerning sexual intercourse and masturbation; but, assuming the sight of a naked body will not rouse universal, uncontrollable desire, sight alone is not a good enough reason for banning a practice. Passers-by can look the other way, and pass by. Our own lives are paramount, to be led as we wish, providing we do not trespass on the lives of others. Live and let live!

Some books, plays, films and speeches may convey unconventional, distasteful, antisocial opinions. They not only illustrate, but actually advocate breaking the basic rules. Society should ignore or dispute them, but silence them only if they are clearly prompting such criminality. Unless and until then, they should not be suppressed, for the sake of freedom. Words should be met with words. Any normal person can see the usefulness of society, and if anyone decides to intimidate or steal or assault he knows what the consequences will be. Somebody may propose antisocial behaviour and be influential, but from the moment we are born society exercises, indeed insists upon, its own influence. We live with it all the time. We also have our own minds, and are capable of considering for ourselves what is presented to us. People should be allowed to state whatever point of view they wish, unless their view is causing, or is on the point of causing not potential but actual, serious harm. Everyone should be as free as possible.

It is sensible and considerate, though, not to cause offence, if it can be avoided without forsaking a significant part of our own freedom. We might moderate our speech and conduct because we would rather not upset others. In some circumstances, reserving one's opinion, struggling for just the right word, and toning down habits would be beneficial all-round. Diplomacy helps harmony.

Some people's actions affect other people indirectly. Commonly, modern society provides not only protection, but also services open to all and paid for by all who can pay. So, for example, if we are ill we expect to be treated. But there are habits and interests, deliberately practised, which encourage illness and injury, such as smoking, over-eating and dangerous sports. Those who don't indulge can rightly object to paying for the treatment of those who do.

There is the whole matter of waste and pollution. Clearly, it is in the interests of all of us to cut them down as much as we can. Fewer and smaller vehicles would be one useful response.

Personal situations can be detrimental to other people – for example, large estates imply less land for the rest of the population, and large families make more demands on local services.

To deal with these matters, smoking, excessively fatty foods and dangerous sports could be banned. There could be rationing, and we could be tempted by financial inducements or even compelled to take exercise. To reduce pollution, cars could be limited to one per household, and their power and mileage restricted; to curb overpopulation, families could be restricted to a certain number of children, and, to provide space, no one allowed more than a certain amount of land unless more was clearly in the public interest, such as for farming. Each of these measures has clear benefits – and clear curtailments of liberty.

It is fair that if one, quite avoidably, takes more than others from a fund, one should contribute more to it, so people who harm or may well harm their health should pay more than those who don't. They would be left with choice, but not at the – literal – expense of others. Where to draw the line and how to charge would have to be decided, but a line should be drawn; an extra charge should be made.

Higher motor tax should be levied on vehicles whose power cannot be justified for practical purposes, and higher council tax expected from large families, who make more use of the services, than small ones, couples or a single person.

Redistributing land entails taking it from some and giving it to others. We could start from scratch and say the landowners took, or were given, too much in the first place. That is a principle. But unless a crime can be shown, the land is legally theirs and to take it without their permission would be theft. Theft can be necessary – as mentioned, taxation. It is also acceptable in extreme situations – a starving man stealing bread – and there may be cases where one person's ownership leaves nothing, or virtually nothing, for anybody else. I understand that technically the British monarchy owns the whole of Britain. The law sanctions another form of theft – compulsory purchase, and there may be circumstances where this is justified, not for convenience but because without it lives would be seriously blighted. But given that 'no stealing' is a fundamental rule of society, society itself should steal only in the most exceptional circumstances.

No killing, no stealing; these are the foundation stones. Safety for self, and for what one owns!

They are negative commands. What of positive ones? If we are in need we appreciate help. A law could be passed: assist, or be punished. But this would go beyond the law's established scope, which is to protect us from, not to look after, one another. Probably, also, it would overstretch duties which are already stretched.

It seems to me that the moral code which is actually and commonly observed is to obey rules, generally; to better our own lives; to be pleasant – at least superficially, and to help a little those who are in need. We recognise the usefulness of society. We would rather have good than bad relationships, and we don't like ourselves or others being in distress. We have some sympathy.

Showing consideration to others may be personally satisfying, and beneficial when we too seek consideration. Perhaps it is asking too much to 'love thy neighbour', but 'to do as you would be done by' remains a sound guide, the best I know, to all-round happiness.

RELIGION

Religion is concerned with beliefs about the explanation and purpose of life. Though any such beliefs are, therefore, religious, traditionally the subject has focused on the supernatural and, in particular, on God.

What is God? Over the centuries God has been thought of as a kind of being, popularly characterised as, 'an old man in the sky'. Some theologians, rejecting this notion as primitive nonsense, have urged us to conceive of God as the absolute, or the ultimate reality, or the supreme reality, or the ground of our being. These definitions are clever, since we can easily recognise them as relating to God, but once stripped of any idea of God as a being, what do they amount to? They suggest something that is fundamental and final, but what can it be? These mighty phrases are, unfortunately, very vacuous. A more informative elaboration is: 'that which we consider to be more important than anything else', but this seems to invite the saying, 'as many men, that many opinions'. Supposing we say our own lives are most important to us. Is this, then, what God means? My life to me, your life to you, and so on? God is each one of us. An unusual conception, at least! The abstract definitions all apply, but still, what is God?

The idea of an old man in the sky is not altogether nonsense. Clearly God is old and located, historically, in heaven, which, traditionally, is in the sky. The real value of likening God to a man is that it illustrates the very widely held, deep-rooted understanding of the word, that God is something conscious, indeed, all-knowing, all-powerful, the creator of everything. Men speak to God in prayer. Accepting this kind of description, but not to be too anthropomorphic, I will take God to mean the supreme being. Does such a being exist?

It has been argued that God's existence can be proved by no more than comprehending the meaning of the word. If he did not exist he would be powerless. But, by definition, he is all powerful.

Therefore, he must exist. We have defined a word in a way that necessarily implies existence, and so to say the word and to deny its existence is to contradict oneself. This, however, is nothing more than just that – words. It is all about verbal constructions. I could imagine a bird, include in its definition that it is able to fly and conclude that it must exist or else it would not be able to fly. Who would believe me? We are looking for existence in fact as well as in thought, for the subject existing 'out there', and that requires sense-experience; perhaps a combination of sense-experience and reason, such as seeing a mark and working out what it might be of.

There have been claims to have seen and/or heard God. Ancient claims raise the suspicion of superstitious minds; modern ones are commonly interpreted as hallucinations. It may well be a case of 'seeing is believing'. Unfortunately, those who have seen cannot convince others in the normal way, by enabling them to see or hear God. Others may or may not be convinced according to their own outlook in general, and their assessment of the claimant and the circumstances in particular. I myself have never experienced such a revelation and I am not prepared to base my own belief on the word of some, no matter how sincerely felt and expressed, since what they are alleging is so unusual. They can describe, but they cannot share, the experience. There is too great a possibility of mistake. I need a personal revelation.

Apart from the normal senses, there is sometimes a reference to a so-called 'sixth sense', not so much of instinct as of certainty; a feeling that without appearing in any form or making any sound, God has impressed himself upon a person. They are convinced. He has substantiated what they have heard and read about him. A scene of nature or a religious service seem to be particularly conducive to this feeling.

If I cannot accept that someone has seen or heard God without me being able to do the same, still less can I accept an appeal to a sense of certainty. I am left wondering if a moving, perhaps awe-inspiring, experience has not been taken too far. The problem remains that the claim cannot be proved by any normal method.

Sometimes believers say that doubters should place themselves in a religious atmosphere or trust or pray, and should the sceptic remain unconvinced, he is not trying hard enough. The believer, it seems, cannot be wrong. Unfortunately, he cannot be shown to be right.

Concerning the existence of God, any call to the senses alone fails since God is not perceived, to universal satisfaction, through the usual senses, as the existence of other entities can, by this means, be demonstrated.

I turn, then, to a combination of sense-experience and rational extension of it.

We live in a world, and we may wonder how it ever came to exist. The question arises because of the principle of causation. We see one thing creating another, like the potter making the pot, and as the pot needs the pot-maker so, we may think, the world needs a world-maker – God. But the pot-maker is himself a creation. So who or what created God?

To say that God created himself is to take the definition of omnipotence to absurdity; that there was God before there was God is a contradiction. While I accept that if there is a god he can turn natural laws upside down, I do not accept, by reason or on trust, that he can reconcile contradictions – these last two words are themselves a contradiction, and if each cancels out the other we are left with nothing.

With cause often comes development. The potter starts with a lump of clay. From an acorn grows an oak tree. The simple becomes more complex. So we trace cause after cause, going back and back until we arrive at as simple a form of substance as we can find. But where did that come from? Again, like God, it could not create itself.

The only alternative to self-creation is that something had no creation, no beginning, it was always there. I can appreciate that there is no beginning to time or space, but the notion that some elements, no matter how minute and simple, were never created and have always existed, leaves me quite perplexed. Given every other substance in the world, I look for a cause. Yet nothing comes from nothing, and self-creation is impossible, so having to choose between a contradiction and a perplexity I choose the perplexity; and bearing in mind the idea of development, supported, indeed, by scientific evidence, I think it is more likely that it was elements that always existed – and developed – than the world as it is now or the most sophisticated being imaginable.

We see patterns in the world, daytime and night-time, seasons and interdependence, and the processes may appear like the workings of a machine: some parts regularly following, some parts regularly interacting with, each other. The world has famously been compared to a watch, and the conclusion drawn that as such an intricate mechanism as a watch requires a maker, it could not have come together by chance, so does the world require a maker – God. Granted that a watch would not be formed by chance, science, however, proposes that our world arose by just that means. The theory is that conditions on earth, unlike any other planet we know of, happened to produce a type of life, and the life evolved over millions of years into the species we have today. Given a favourable atmosphere and chemical fusion, the rest followed. There was no need for God. Leaving evolution aside, still I can see particles and forces interacting and producing without God.

A watch does not allow for growth, which we find within and all around us, the simple becoming complex, suggesting development rather than arrangement of completed parts was our real history. Watches display an intricacy which the world does not; the earth revolving around the sun at a constant rate being the limit of our natural precision; the seasons arising from this happening. Fundamentally, two objects in unison, not many! And a watch has a clear purpose, which the world does not.

Supernatural occurrences provide arguments for the existence of God. These challenge us to explain not the natural world, but the unnatural features of it.

Consider miracles of healing: if someone is ill and an appeal is made to God to cure him and he is cured, then it is claimed, reasonably, that God has cured him and, therefore, there is a god.

First, we need to verify the event, to establish that the person really was ill and really was cured without any sort of medical intervention or by the natural cessation of the illness. It must be clear that the illness stopped unnaturally. Assuming there is no normal explanation, still God is not the only answer.

There are the awkward claims of non-believers being miraculously cured by the thoughts, and perhaps the touching, of other non-believers who maintain that sometimes at least they are able to heal in this way though they don't know how they do it. Perhaps they make a mental impact which influences the physical condition.

This raises the possibility of psychosomatic healing. Clearly our minds do affect our bodies; indeed, usually they dictate what our bodies do. For example, I may wish to write; my hand duly picks up a pen. Various emotions often carry physical connotations, nervousness and distress, relief and joy, for instance. There are cases of people forcing their bodies through extraordinary feats, including overcoming life-threatening and debilitating conditions. The psychosomatic argument is that if a healing occurs, without natural causes, it is the mind of the subject, perhaps in conjunction with another mind, not God's, which is responsible. Such an extension of mind over matter may seem hard to accept, but so is the notion that the healing was performed by an invisible being.

I will digress from the existence of God to the existence of life after death since belief in the afterlife may make it easier to believe in God. In looking for evidence, I think of ghosts. If they exist then some people at least survive death.

As with seeing or hearing God, there would be nothing like personal experience. What we have are anecdotes, though some include difficulties for the doubter, such as a claim that the ghost revealed information that the onlooker would not have known without the revelation. Considering such stories, we wonder about an overactive imagination, a persuasive atmosphere, a visual or more general error, or outright deception. If the alleged sighting really does throw up a problem we expect others with more time and, frankly, more dedication, to investigate and publicise it. To prove the existence of ghosts really would be a scoop. But they have not been established to general satisfaction, while the proposition that at death our bodies release some ethereal form of ourselves, with its own life, is incredible.

A recent argument for life after death is post-death glimpses of another life. Modern medicine is able to bring some people back from the dead, to the extent that their heart has stopped and is restarted. Sometimes such patients report having had experiences while dead, such as leaving their bodies and adopting a new form of body, looking down at attempts to revive them, meeting deceased relatives, travelling through a tunnel, encountering a father-like figure who reviews their life, emerging into an attractive setting, meeting more former relatives, then being drawn back to their original body as it is resuscitated.

What these stories may stem from are memories, in the early stages, and dreams, full of expectations, before death closes both. We are well acquainted with the ideas of judgement and heaven. If anything is to happen after death this is what many people expect to happen. Realising their condition is serious, they are likely to be concentrating on such concepts.

One definite argument for these experiences is the claim that patients can describe, in detail, their resuscitation. Their account can be compared to the event itself. In considering their stories however, we should remember that scenes of resuscitation are commonly shown in films and on television, so that many of us have some idea of the procedure. Secondly, in regaining life the patient's level of consciousness may well fluctuate, and for moments he may be near enough conscious to receive and retain snippets of information. There is also the issue of 'heart dead' and 'brain-dead.' Though the heart dies, is the brain, for a short time, still receptive? As with ghosts, convincing evidence is required, and, again, the basic idea that at death we take on a new form of life and, in this case, reside in paradise, is incredible.

I have considered claims for the existence of God, and for life after death, and found them insufficient for belief: God cannot be revealed by words alone; it is more rational to accept an eternal particle than an eternal being, and exceptional interaction rather than external design; religious experience is too subjective, miracles more likely to be explained psychologically than supernaturally, and ghosts and post-death accounts too unnatural and questionable.

There are problems with the characteristics of God. If he is self-sufficient, why did he create a world at all? If he is loving, why did he create a world which, in its very nature, is unloving, where one form of life can only survive by killing another, and which contains deadly, structural features such as earthquakes, bearing in mind God is also all-powerful? The answer that some people committed sin and were punished with a brutal world raises not only a question of history, but also of justice. Why should we suffer for their sin? The next answer, that sooner or later we too will sin since the fault is in us, smacks of sadism, especially considering the doctrine that in any case we will be judged. So why not let us live in a world which in its natural state is good, and if we personally are bad we personally will suffer for it?

We live for a few decades, if that. Why, then, should the reward or punishment last for ever?

Can an animal sin? If not, it should not be punished. Yet an antelope, for example, lives in fear of a lion. Such is God's world.

How can many people be blamed for not believing – a person, for instance, who has learned something about religious beliefs, but grows up in a country that insists they are wrong?

Considering the array of aspects that comprise a life, the needs, desires, personality, influences and demands, a multitude of situations and interactions, how can many of us be judged, overall, as good or bad? Overall, we are a great mixture.

A believer might say, trust God. Have faith! But I cannot trust God before I have decided there is a god.

I start with what I know, and when I am introduced to the concept of God I ask is it more reasonable to believe in him than not to believe in him? I conclude that it is likely that God does not exist.

So I am an atheist, but a reluctant, not a rabid, one. I would rather be a believer – who wouldn't, faced with the grave or heaven?

Theism is a belief, for the most part, honestly held. Atheism is a belief, for the most part, honestly held. No one can demonstrate – to the point that all ordinary people would accept – that there is or isn't a god, or that there is or isn't life after death. When we die, we have the answer, but at that point, of course, either we can't recognise it, because we can't recognise anything, or, if we can, we can't convey it to universal satisfaction.

I turn, briefly, to some facets of faith in practice, concentrating upon Christianity, because it is the religion I know best, though I think the issues raised apply, to some extent, to other religions too.

Jesus taught that we should love our enemies; if struck, we should turn the other cheek. Why, then, is Christianity blamed for some wars? Simply, people start wars, and people don't always follow the teaching; as well as love they also feel hate, greed, ambition, zeal and righteous indignation.

'Zeal' and 'righteous indignation' are barbed topics.

Jesus told his disciples to spread the word. Christianity is missionary, and many have preached it fervently. Sometimes it has been forced upon individuals and societies, and sometimes Christians have fought between themselves and persecuted each other because they have insisted on the observance of their own, particular interpretations. Quite sickening tortures and executions have been carried out in the name of the true faith, and those responsible could claim a clear conscience, saying it did not matter what you did to the body so long as you saved the soul.

Jesus never advocated belief at the point of a sword. When he sent his disciples out to preach he said that if any town rejected them they were to move on – though not without a symbolic warning.

If you hold a belief dearly, you are naturally offended if that belief is insulted. To what extent you display your feelings depends on personal temperament, morality and judgement. Jesus himself drove the traders out of the temple, overturning their tables and stools.

I can appreciate why the crusaders were incensed by Muslims occupying the Holy Land. A religion which denied the divinity of Jesus and extolled another as its prophet was proclaiming itself in the very country where Jesus once walked. Think of the outcry, then and now, if Christians controlled Mecca.

Today, thankfully, there is more of a spirit of tolerance. People are expected – indeed commanded – to show respect to other faiths, so there is less chance of causing offence, and less still of persecution and war.

If there is a war, no matter what the cause or the aim, it is likely God will be dragged into it. Each side claims he is on its side.

The church had leaders. They were important. Historically, many were politically as well as spiritually important, and it is all too natural that many went the way of the world, concerned with power and possessions, appearing more like earthly princes than heavenly saints.

Jesus too considered himself important, indeed, the most important of all. But he shunned the way of the world. He did not seek some official role. He preached that possessions were a dangerous distraction.

As I wander around a cathedral, marvelling at its grandeur, I sometimes think, wouldn't it have been better to have spent the labour and the money devoted on it, to assisting those who were in need? I appreciate, though, the desire to give what one can to what one loves, to indicate the majesty of God, to fortify his followers. If kings lived in palaces, should not the king of kings? Understandable, if misguided.

Christianity has been criticised for reconciling millions to their miserable existence. No matter that you are suffering now – you will be rewarded in heaven. But not everyone stops with a smile and a pat on the head. Innumerable acts of kindness have been performed because of Christian convictions. 'Love thy neighbour' in practice! 'The Good Samaritan' taken to heart! Think of the charities that stand on Christian foundations.

Heaven or hell or neither? It is our ultimate gamble. I have chosen atheism because my thoughts lead to it. But if I am wrong the consequences may be terrible, and if I am right the only point of life becomes whatever point I give it, and death – not some form of sleep, but a loss of every sensation for evermore – really is the end.

My deeds may leave a speck of influence. I will be remembered by a few. But I will know nothing of it, and soon any influence, and the memories, will fade away. I will be completely forgotten. The famous are recorded, but they too shrink, even in the textbooks, as time rolls on. Such are our lives, and such may well be the fate of all life on earth – oblivion.

In the meantime, here I sit. An intriguing question emerges: if a belief, true or false, makes you happier, is it worth believing?

POLITICS

Politics is concerned with government, that is, a person or people deciding the laws and policies of a society. Without such direction, there would be not society, but autonomous individuals – anarchy – and the fear of anarchy is insecurity, warfare and brutish domination. So, according to theory, the individual gives up some of his autonomy in the belief that overall his life will be better inside, rather than outside, society. Still, in the main, he will be dominated, but by law, to which he contributes, not by the whim of the strongest person.

The whole system provides protection, even against itself, as well as obligation. The law can be used against the government. Checks and balances!

Each person wishes to hold onto his personal life, and the aspects of it are enshrined as his natural rights, implying that they are connected to nature, perhaps recalling the freedom of it, or a common deep desire of human nature, or 'nature' as in 'naturally', meaning 'obvious'.

Not God-given nor pre-existing, natural rights are the results of our reflections upon our feelings, wishes and expectations balanced against the demands of living socially. They usually include the right to life itself, to form a belief, to hold an opinion and to exercise a preference, to own possessions, to choose a form of employment, to marry and start a family and to regulate one's own home life.

As a member of society, the citizen expects to adhere to the general will, providing it does not infringe upon his natural rights, but he also expects to be part of the forming of that will – he is part of his society, he entered it like others and he is like others. Therefore, he too should have a say, usually expressed through a vote. Moreover, his vote should count as much as the next. We are fundamentally the same, so we should be treated the same.

Some people have more status, wealth and intelligence than others, and are more knowledgeable about a certain subject, but if, for these reasons we give more importance to some – to whom, precisely? How much more importance? Two votes? Two hundred? Two thousand? An interminable debate seems to be in prospect.

Concentrating upon wealth in particular, income tax could be used as a benchmark – the more tax you pay the more votes you have, because the more you are contributing to the national budget. Certainly this would be one way – and a reasonable way – of rewarding the higher taxpayers. But there would still be the problems of drawing the dividing lines and deciding how many extra votes.

A moral issue would arise about those who contribute to society in a very useful, but less pecuniary manner – volunteers, for example. There is the danger of groups growing powerful enough to overwhelm the wishes of others.

Apart from the difficulties, status, wealth and intelligence are, strictly, irrelevant to the political process. Given an issue, each of us chooses an option, preferred probably for our own personal reasons. We are expressing our opinion and since opinions are, by their nature, subjective, grounded on our own sense of what is important, then, providing a view is not largely based upon a demonstrable falsehood, one person's opinion is as valid as another's. Politically, we are equal.

Legally, too, we are equal. Society cannot tolerate any crime; one major reason for its existence is to protect its members, and justice – which is a legal name for fairness – demands that each person is subject to the same legal procedure and consequences.

Political equality excludes oligarchies and dictatorships since they deny political power to some or all of their population. These systems are, by nature, repressive – to the point of replacing free speech by enforced speech. If they were to allow open debate, sooner or later there would be criticism, alternatives would be proposed which might become popular, and the rule of the elite would be threatened.

For each individual to retain as much freedom as possible, and to be as powerful as possible, there is only one form of government – democracy, one person one vote. Then, given that on most matters there are different opinions, and so different votes, only one of which can be chosen, the preference of the majority is decisive since it satisfies the largest number of people.

I do not know how societies actually emerged, but I suggest that the theory I have outlined makes sense historically. Starting with families, for societies to have arisen, families must have united. There may have been some subjugation, but if one family bound another in a master/slave relationship then, I conjecture, this enforced unity would have broken down at the first opportunity, and the subdued would have escaped into the ample freedom all around to renew their independence. Within a family there may well have been a dominant individual whom other members were accustomed, but not compelled like slaves, to follow. If they joined a society and regretted it, they could have left.

The general pattern, it seems to me, would probably have been for the individuals in one family to agree to unite with the individuals in another, for pleasure and for protection, and to live under a common code. So the unity would have been, by and large, voluntary.

Nowadays we are born into long-established countries. We are never asked if we agree to become citizens; indeed, if we wanted to opt out it would be difficult to find a spot on the planet not claimed by one nation or another. We are, in the event, enclosed in some society throughout our lives, whether or not we choose to be.

The fundamental problem for democracy is that these countries are huge, containing millions of people, which makes it impractical for the population to vote upon all proposed policies and laws; that would require constant organisation and the results would be slow.

We see how busy parliament is. Imagine the work and time required if the business had to be deliberated not by hundreds, but by millions. What if there was an emergency requiring an immediate response?

Many people could not spare hours to consider proposals, and many would not want to – I am mindful that some find voting once in five years too much.

If citizens do not wish to participate that is their decision and they should not be forced. The issues will be decided by those who are prepared to be involved, but these men and women cannot be expected, in addition to their normal lives, to review all the proposed policies and legislation that would be presented. It would be too much.

Countries that retain vestiges of democracy commonly ask their citizens, every few years, to choose representatives who form the legislature and the government. Such a system might more accurately be called 'representocracy'.

It seems unlikely that nation states will decentralise into city and rural ones, and practise real democracy. I doubt that they would change voluntarily, and the only other way I can see this arising is as a result of some universal catastrophe, such as a devastating world war, leaving far fewer people and a breakdown of central authority. Moreover, city-states could attract aggression. Overcoming a city might be less daunting than overcoming a country, and the conquered could lose all political power. If city-states were to exist, men would need to curb their greed.

Assuming, though, that countries and populations remain much the same as they are at present, the aim is to make them as democratic as possible, to give each person as much power as can be managed, to draw theory and practice as close together as can be achieved.

Three steps towards democracy would be:

Firstly, to remember always that representatives represent the will of the majority of their electorate, not just in its choice of candidate but also in its opinion on the matters of the day, and that is most days, not only those around election time. They are not simply to take voters' views into account, but to air, support and, in turn, vote themselves for those views. They are mouth-pieces: otherwise they may thwart the wishes and certainly the power of the people.

This, of course, makes those who are elected appear to be puppets, which is not an attractive role. But they have their own opinions, which they can argue as much as anyone, and these are likely to be particularly noted because of their position. They can threaten to resign if they really disagree and their electorate might not want to lose them, and, as stated, since the people will not be involved in all matters there will be occasions – probably many – when the representative has to judge their wishes as best he can.

Secondly, referendums – where the electorate itself directly decides a question – instead of being extremely rare, should be as common as possible.

Thirdly, elections to parliament should be held more than once every five years. I have no definite time in mind, but I am inclined to think of three years, and no more than four. The principle is that the people should judge a parliament when it has had a chance to prove itself.

So each adult votes for a spokesperson. Again, given the sheer size of countries and the wish for each person's preference to make an impact, it is likely that hundreds of representatives would be elected. They pass laws and pursue policies according to the general opinion of their electors.

As far as feasible, the representatives themselves form the government; other tiers being added only if needed, such as the appointment of individuals to ensure that policies are carried out, or to meet an immediate crisis. Any post-holders should be chosen by the people or, with the people's permission, by parliament.

I am not trying to write a constitution, and I am aware of at least some of the questions that would arise if my proposals were pressed into detail; for example, given that it is not practical for the public to participate in all political processes, which matters should be left to their representatives? How do the representatives learn of their electorates' views? What should be the maximum length of one parliament? How many post-holders are necessary? Then there would be many more questions about procedures and timings. Ultimately, the people themselves should provide the answers by choosing options.

What I am maintaining is that to return as much as possible to democracy, people need to be involved as much as possible in the political process. I see more opportunity for this than is practised at the moment.

One feature of modern 'democracies' is political parties. These seem to be taken for granted, to the point that we grow up assuming they are needed for democracy to function at all. Individuals with an interest in politics feel obliged to join a party and, indeed, as it is, so they must if they seek political power. The conflicting ideas, on principles and particulars, and the open debates certainly illustrate democratic behaviour.

However, far from being necessary to, political parties are an imposition upon, democracy. They are not needed. Each person can debate values and policies and come to his own conclusion. Instead of asking our views and acting upon them, political parties draw up their own agendas and ask us to sign up to them. Of course it is to be hoped that they have contacted some of the public and taken their feelings into account, and, indeed, arrived at their own decisions by democratic means; but they have not given all of the public an opportunity to register their opinions, and they are not committed to enacting the majority opinion. They are so dominant and pervasive they expect a person to bend to whichever party comes nearest to his outlook. An unnatural tail wagging the dog!

Parties field their own candidates and, reasonably, expect them to follow party policy, not necessarily the electorate's wishes. There may be times when the representative considers that what his party wants is not what his electorate wants. He must choose between being undemocratic and being disloyal, and the latter may jeopardise his career.

Under the present practice the party that wins the most con-stituencies forms the government, and the others the opposition. It is most likely that the opposition will be outvoted on many occasions, and the wishes of their electorate will also be defeated.

Without parties the people themselves set the agenda, and though their views may differ from place to place and issue to issue, the dividing lines will not be so clearly drawn and the outcomes not so predictable, and, hopefully, more people will see their wishes approved more often. The very concept of opposition encourages polarisation, criticism for the sake of it, to justify the name, opposition.

Successful parties claim a mandate to enact all of their mani-festo, though many people who voted for them may well have voted for only some of it. Without parties, manifestos would come directly from the electorate. They would be local between each constituency and its representative, who would then argue for the points within Parliament.

I think it more likely that political parties will break down than that nations will. I detect a blurring of beliefs, even of names, and among voters affiliations do not seem to be so entrenched, as divisions within society are themselves more blurred.

Given countries and representatives, we can still move towards democracy by, firstly, concentrating on representatives as individuals, asking which, regardless of party name, is most likely to do what we want them to do; secondly, by we ourselves deciding as many matters as possible; and, thirdly, by choosing our parliaments more often.

Such is the spirit of democracy, and though practicalities may call for trimmings, the people – who by the definition of democracy *are* the government – should participate in politics as much as they can, make their concerns and opinions very clear, and, providing it does not tread on individual rights, their general opinion should be supreme.

SOCIALISM AND CAPITALISM

I understand socialism to mean especially concerned with people in general, and capitalism to mean especially concerned with individuals in particular. Socialism emphasises the many, and so, equality; capitalism the one, and so, liberty. Both are laudable. Each can exterminate the other.

Equality can become uniformity, so that people live, look and even think the same. Then they are as robots. Liberty can lead to a few people becoming extremely prosperous while millions of others strive to keep themselves alive.

Historically, socialism has focussed on the poor. Its aim has been to raise their standard of living. This may be achieved at the expense of the rich. It is natural for socialists to charge the wealthy with lack of compassion, and to regard them with some disdain. By definition – its stress on what is common to all – and by inclination – its wish to reduce differences – socialism is, to some extent, a leveller.

But, in many ways, people are not all on the same level; some are more intelligent and strong than others; they are more able; some spend, others save and so, eventually, the savers can afford something better; some strike lucky, others not. To restrain a person's capabilities is to violate their personality, their own life; and to deprive them of what they have legitimately gained is to steal. Within basic, social laws a person should be free to prosper.

Socialism and capitalism! To what extent can the merits in both ideologies be harmonised?

One advantage of living in a society is, or should be, personal safety. We abide by a code and expect to be protected by it. Given that we are all much the same, it is reasonable, and generally accepted, that we should be treated the same. So each of us is equal before the law. Some characteristics of life, primarily life itself, and some values, such as dignity and choice, are declared to be rights. They are so fundamental they can be claimed by all. No one should take them away. In so-called democracies there is the principle of one person, one vote. To this extent there is, or should be, equality.

For individuality, there is good reason for personal possessions. We may grow or make or buy something. Then we may fairly call it ours. It is our return for our labour or our expenditure. It is ours by right.

There are items which, though not absolutely necessary for life, certainly help to sustain it. One of them is a shelter. Of course we could huddle under trees, assuming some are available, but this would be inefficient and uncomfortable to the point of incurring illness and threatening life. So we build or buy shelters for ourselves. They stand on land, so that piece of land becomes ours, and into what we call our home we bring furniture and utensils. We wear clothes. Having been gained by fair means, these are our own possessions. Would we wish it otherwise? Would we prefer nobody owning anything, so we take anything from each other, and move on to and off all land, and in to and out of all property, whenever we wish? The problem is not ownership itself, but when a few own so much that others are left in poverty.

Overseeing the country is the state. Since it is concerned with everyone it is, by definition, socialistic. It supervises its society, primarily protecting its citizens from attack from each other, and from other countries. If there is a shortage of food or water, there will probably be disturbances. Desperate people may resort to crime. It is the state's duty to prevent crime, but to do so without addressing such a basic cause as hunger would not only be inhumane, but also self-defeating. Dire need is ever likely to result in dire action.

Of far less importance, but still important, is the supply of light and heat, in the form of electricity and gas, and the building and maintenance of networks of travel. These conveniences exist, and people expect them; their lives, and the nation's economy, would be severely disrupted without them.

Many governments wish their citizens to be content; that is good in itself, it is popular, a mark of success and a source of pride. A strong economy gives power and influence, respect and status. All very desirable!

So the state is drawn into more than preventing crime and invasion. Basic commodities and utilities may be provided privately, but should one fail the consequences would be so serious the state would have to step in anyway; if it at least regulates them, it guards against breakdown, and exploitation, and gives a sense of security. Therefore the state increases its influence overall, and becomes more socialistic.

Sometimes we fall ill; we injure ourselves; we may develop a serious disease. Treatment can be expensive, perhaps more than we can afford. Are we to be left to suffer and die? We may fall on hard times, and become virtually penniless. Are we to be left to the elements and the begging bowl until, again, we succumb? For our own sakes, and for the sakes of others, a feeling of pity, and a desire to help, many of us welcome the welfare state. It provides another form of most valuable protection – a safety net!

Education offers a more interesting life, and is vital to modern society. Anyone who is illiterate and innumerate is at a great disadvantage in their day-to-day activities, and in their prospects of employment. Without education our society would regress, and in various ways we would become the poorer.

Though education is not a natural right, an inseparable expression of one's self, but an enhancement of one's life, I favour everyone being educated, children compulsorily, for their own benefit and for the benefit of society. More influence by the state! More equality! More socialism!

Sometimes it is proposed that health and education are so important there should be nothing but state schemes, for private ones give users too much of an advantage. Every day, of course, people gain over each other by many means, in many respects, but it is claimed that in health and education the advantages are lifelong, which is going too far.

Anybody who is rich can lead a more comfortable life than somebody who is not, and for so long as they have wealth, which could be for life. So should we forbid anyone becoming rich? Some people will always have more than others, if only because some save and others spend.

The social code demands that we should not harm others, and providing we don't, freedom demands we should be allowed to lead our own lives as we wish, which includes spending our own money as we wish. Does spending some of it on our health and education cause harm, and sufficient to justify prohibiting such expenditure?

Private practice may cause, very indirectly, some harm. In medicine it may provide not better, but quicker treatment, aggravate waiting lists and use time and resources which otherwise would be spent on the National Health Service. In education it may raise a pupil to a standard he would not attain ordinarily and so make him a stronger candidate for employment than a rival who cannot afford similar schooling. In medicine, though, I understand there is a strict demarcation between private and national health practice, so that private patients do not jump the queue but form a separate one, and staff treating them work outside of their stipulated National Health Service schedule. In education, so much depends on personality, ability, motivation and sheer luck; private schools provide smaller classes and concentrated timetables. A state pupil can – and many do – bridge the gap.

Any advantage gained by buying care and education does not outweigh our right to control our own spending, our natural desire to look after ourselves and the social tenet that we should indeed look after ourselves, providing we do not really harm others.

A person should be able to start and run his own business. He sets his conditions of employment, and potential employees accept them or go elsewhere. Likewise, potential customers accept his prices or shop elsewhere. But a number of employers could band together and insist on very low wages or very high prices. This could cause hardship and suffering. Where there is no other competition, the government itself could set up similar businesses and compete; but this would be a drain on national resources, a diversion from important affairs, and it would take time, during which the deprivations would continue and increase. The government could make good the difference in wages and prices, but this would be exploited by unscrupulous employers.

I therefore favour the state curbing employers who are exploiting the public. It could ban monopolies altogether, but they might not all be bad. Wages sinking and prices spiralling are the concerns, and the obvious way of ensuring that they do not is to fix a minimum wage and a maximum price. Prices, however, might rise for reasons a businessman cannot control, and it would be absurd to expect him to operate at a loss, so what would need to be regulated is not prices, but profit.

The government has an estimate of what it costs to live tolerably, and the minimum wage could be set accordingly.

Unless businesses supply the details, the government will not know the cost of production of every object, but it, or local administration, could check prices, the public assisting by reporting suspicious rises, and the authorities could order a reduction of any price which was excessive. What would be reduced would be profit. The law would be saying that profit over a certain amount is just too much, in its impact on the consumer and, through its impact on the cost of living, on everyone. If the producer did not comply, he would be prosecuted.

So, exploitation becomes a crime. It is not stealing, since the loser is agreeing to his loss, but he is agreeing because he has no realistic alternative. His acceptance is against his wishes. Exploitation is akin to stealing.

Safety standards are required to protect employees from danger. Again people have a choice – stay or leave – but if they want to work, they may have no choice; and, again, the state cannot ignore its citizens being harmed, nor always be able to provide an alternative.

Whereas an employee may leave his employment for any reason he wishes, he may not be told to leave without a very grave reason, such as misconduct or incompetence. Strictly, this is unfair on the employer. He may, for example, find or think that he could find somebody better. Generally, though, it is far more serious for a person to be without a job than for a business to be without that person. Therefore, I am in favour of employees retaining their security – and, indeed, their freedom to leave – providing they do their work satisfactorily.

Sometimes it is decided that a particular job is no longer needed, or cannot be afforded, and the person who has been doing it becomes redundant. Unfortunate though this is, there is no justification for an employer having to make a redundancy payment, usually according to the number of years the person has worked for the company – more years, more money. An owner may give a good worker a gift, out of gratitude, but he should not be legally obliged to give him anything except the conditions agreed in the contract and a period of notice sufficient for the worker to try and obtain another job.

A person may buy land, primarily for his home, and of course a very rich person can buy a great deal of land. This could cause hardship by compelling other people to live in overcrowded conditions. Another problem is that someone's land, or a part of it, may become the obvious site for a much-needed facility, such as a hospital, or for a road to link or divert increasing traffic. The state may insist on compulsory purchase which, because it is overruling rights to own land and to be the legitimate owner, should be the last resort; but because without the additional amenity the community will suffer, and assuming that the owner is compensated and assisted in full, compulsory purchase should be a possible resort.

So, if the state extends its basic function of protecting its citizens from attack to protecting them in general, it forbids not only violence and theft, but also some seemingly legitimate situations which actually have harmful impacts. It clips individual freedoms, turning aspects of them into crimes, if it considers they are causing hardship.

The state is naturally socialistic – concerned with all – and the more it is concerned, the more socialistic it is; the less it involves itself, the more an individual can flourish, at the expense of others if he himself does not have a social conscience.

Government has to be paid for, and a welfare system requires more payment. Since it supplies to all in the same degree, it should be paid for by all in the same amount. Income tax, therefore, is unjust. One should not pay more if one does not receive more. Here, however, I declare a prejudice. I am glad of income tax because I think it likely that the money taken will be better spent than if it is left with its owner. The government, hopefully, will spend it on need; the owner may well spend it on personal luxuries.

We are all, by nature, selfish and, given the means, we are all, from time to time, self-indulgent, but habitual self-indulgence is, by my values, too selfish considering the suffering in the world; the starvation and the cruelty that is the lot of millions. To lavish on oneself as much luxury as possible implies a lack of regard for the rest of mankind. Surely we can agree that saving a life comes before being pampered? Not that this will always be uppermost in our minds; we all want to live in some comfort, and to 'splash out' occasionally, but bearing in mind the plight of others, we may baulk at living sumptuously. However, if anyone does not share my qualms, that is his choice. Within the law everyone should be able to spend their own money as they wish. Naturally! I view a spendthrift lifestyle as contemptible, but also, as a right, untouchable.

Materialism! All around success is measured by wealth – the size of the house, the make of the car, and so on and so on. Riches earn status. 'Haves' and 'have nots' create class division, traditionally the upper, middle and lower classes, with those beneath paying deference to those above. Though wealth remains a common goal, my impression is that with the rise of notions like free speech, equality and socialism, of trade unions and skilled workers demanding high payments, there is less division and less deference now.

Countries too have sought to show that they are important by erecting ornate buildings and staging lavish ceremonies. These exhibits and displays also, I think, have declined. In general, nations seem to be less ostentatious and more utilitarian, enabling more to be spent on the welfare of the living. These days when some spectacle is proclaimed somebody is likely to point out how many hospitals could be built instead, and I murmur my assent.

I am not a killjoy, but if we care about the suffering in the world and knowing that money will make a difference, we will restrict how much we spend on ourselves, preferring to give some of the excess to the needy rather than wallow in sheer extravagance.

The welfare state tries to ensure that none of its citizens actually suffer. It provides basic utilities, health and education services, and housing, employment and financial assistance. What if somebody does not wish to participate in some or all of the welfare? He must support the state itself, that is, live under its laws and contribute financially to its defence, or leave its boundaries, but if he wants and is able to provide or pay for any aspect of welfare himself he should be allowed to do so, since these aspects are not of the essence of society itself. If he opts out it should be made clear that he will be charged if, at any time, he opts in, but while he is out he should not be charged as though he is in. It is simpler to tax everyone, but unfair to tax anyone for what he does not receive. Once again, however, I declare a prejudice: if the rich pay publicly as well as privately, there is more for society as a whole.

Equality! Yet natural characteristics show, and freedom allows for, some inequality. Care! Yet if two people aim for the same goal there will be selfishness and competition. Each concept has its place. We should have equality in our rights and before the law. Where there is a welfare state – and I would like one everywhere – it is for the benefit of all, though if anyone wishes to provide for himself privately he should be able to do so. Everyone may own personal possessions, including land; in extreme circumstances, however, the state may insist on purchasing the land. An individual can set up his own business, mostly on his own terms, but there must be safety standards, and there will be laws on wages and profits to prevent exploitation and hardship. Having paid his dues, a person's money is his own. He decides what to do with it. This is my blend of socialism and capitalism.

HUMANS AND OTHER LIFE

It is natural and evident that life forms of all sorts focus on themselves. Where there is consciousness, each wishes to survive, and, usually, to dwell among its own kind, in some form of community.

As men advanced far beyond all other life they made their whole species special. For themselves they created morals and laws and rights; human beings were what mattered, though at various times, in various ways, sharp distinctions have been drawn between them.

Generally – Eastern religions are a glowing exception – men have regarded other species as quite different and quite inferior, treated them as objects, and used them for their own benefit, extending consideration only in so far as it served human purposes. This attitude grew naturally, from the affinities between mankind, the obvious differences from other life, and the need for survival. It was taken beyond necessity into convenience, such as riding horses; comfort, such as wearing furs; sport and profit; it was ingrained and unquestioned. I have read that when animal welfare for the sake of the animals was first introduced in the House of Commons it was met with laughter, so strange and absurd was the idea!

The basic reason for man's overall superiority is that we are able to think more comprehensively than other forms of life – not that other creatures cannot think or communicate, but man can do both better. Most differences between humans and other species are of degree, not kind, with one being better in some respects and another in other respects. An elephant, for example, is stronger than a man, though both have strength.

Whatever the differences, of kind or degree, we do not make specific characteristics the criteria in affording rights. Humans are not granted life, protection, liberty, equality and dignity according to, say, how clever or strong or helpful they are. If attributes were pivotal, the more useful the more rights, a dog would have more than, for instance, a mentally handicapped person. To make capabilities all-important for rights would be superficial, since we share fundamentals, and contentious – what capabilities, and how much of each for which rewards?

Humans have their status simply because they are human, an amalgamation of similarity, selfishness and superiority, all very understandable. However, to be concerned only with ourselves and to disregard and exploit other forms of life is quite excessively selfish, as it would be if one person treated other people in this way. It is also unreasonable – as we afford rights to ourselves, despite our differences, it is consistent and fair that we should afford rights to other kinds, despite their more obvious, but outward, differences. All life is much the same in needs, and all sentient life much the same in desires.

The starting point is what we find and how we react to it – we find living entities indicating that they want to live, contentedly. The natural, moral conclusion is, then let them live, contentedly, so far as is possible.

I say, 'so far as is possible.' We find another fact, a horrible one: each kind lives by killing and eating another; it has to, to survive. Killing is not just a way, but the way of life. Humans have organised the process professionally: farms, abattoirs, butchers and grocers, though with a sense of morality and a technological skill we can reduce the scope and the suffering. The day may even dawn when we are able to exist entirely on substances that have died naturally, or been created artificially.

Since life with feeling wishes to live, attention has turned to life without feeling, such as vegetables, and many people are vegetarians. If it is shown that, in fact, vegetables have feelings of sorts, still we need to eat something; and if that has to be killed, then that which has little awareness and appreciation experiences less and loses less than that which has more. We give priority to whatever has most to lose. So, better to kill a cabbage than a cow! This is also one argument for not killing and eating each other.

Cabbages and suchlike, though, may not satisfy all our nutri-tional needs, and we may have to take from further up the food chain – morally, only so far as is necessary. Yet other factors, such as taste, variety and custom, though not essential, could be very influential, and incline us to eat an animal. Then, for those who recognise a dilemma at all, there is a conflict between morality, health and desire. I look forward to the day, and I think it will come, when animals are not reared for meat, and I am not tempted and do not succumb. The law could lay down boundaries. At present only humans seem to be off the menu.

Self-defence is another reason for killing. We may be attacked by something wishing to make us its food. Ideally we should try to deter, not kill, but if a confrontation comes to the point of us or them, naturally we place ourselves first.

There are some forms of life inherently harmful to us, such as germs, malignant cells and some insects – mosquitoes, for example. Again, the ideal is to keep out, not wipe out, but, again, killing could be the only way of stopping the harm which could itself be deadly; though if it is not, the issue arises of whether we are prepared to tolerate some discomfort, even pain, rather than take a life.

Normally, we are more ready to kill microbes or insects than animals. Insects are small, often tiny, with few discernible features and no visible facial expressions. We don't like the feel of them. An aesthetic distinction is drawn between, say, butterflies, which we find beautiful, and, say, spiders, which we find ugly. Insects can be killed instantly, without causing distress on either side, and that is the simplest way of getting rid of them, but it is also taking a life unnecessarily.

Animals are more like us, larger and so everything about them is more obvious. We see clearly that they have a face and expressive eyes. They can be affectionate. In pain they cry out, and they shed blood. Humans feel pity, a wish to relieve suffering and save from death. Perhaps the surest way to become a vegetarian is to visit an abattoir.

Men have developed a code of conduct, classed acts as good and bad. Morality! They have also agreed that kindness is to be applauded; cruelty, deplored. To inflict pain where it can be avoided is wrong, and to feel some pleasure from inflicting it is sadistic. Sadists are evil, if not insane.

It is contrary to the values we apply to ourselves, and sometimes speak of as absolutes, not to regard all life with respect, recognising and, so far as it is possible, preserving its wish to live, and without disturbance.

Selfishness beyond necessity will probably always intrude, at times for powerful and persuasive reasons, but we should realise that it is fundamentally wrong, since there is nothing more important than life. In essence, all life is the same and so, logically, should be treated the same. We teach consideration and compassion, and we are upset by pain and distress, and try to help.

In depriving anything of a right to live we are taking away its primary right, all that it possesses. Such an act should be seen for what it is, a tragedy, and when we do something we would rather not, we feel distaste, regret, unhappiness. Therefore to treat the taking of life as entertainment, as a sport, is a dreadful perversion, which means those who act in this way are truly perverts. I wonder if people who dress themselves up, and set out to kill an animal or watch it being killed, in party atmosphere, have ever considered just what they are doing; or whether they are mind-lessly continuing a tradition which once enjoyed the sight of men stabbing each other to death in an arena. Moreover, there is the suffering. Fox-hunting, deer hunting and hare coursing cause sheer, prolonged terror to the creature until, having run for its life, it is caught or collapses exhausted and is ripped to pieces.

A particularly horrendous so-called sport is bullfighting because the bull is deliberately and repeatedly tortured before it is killed – chased through the streets, beaten as it runs, its horns blunted, its eyes smeared to blur its vision, its neck muscles cut, all for the safety of the public. Then some woefully misguided man, extravagantly attired for the occasion, sticks spear after spear into the animal until eventually it dies, though not before its ears are cut off, as trophies!

Fiesta days are marked by other obscenities: bulls are dragged in once more, this time to have their horns set on fire, or to be pushed under water until they drown; goats are thrown from the tops of high buildings, such as churches of all places; chickens are hung on lines and young girls hack at them with swords; the girls are blindfolded and the swords are smoothed, just to prolong the fun.

If a person conducted anything like these practices upon another person, society would be sickened and shocked. The perpetrator would be branded inhuman, a monster, a psychopath, and locked away for life. Can we not see that the victims are like us? They too feel pain. They too want to live, happily. Politicians should be condemned for allowing these barbarities to continue within their borders.

Fishing, as a pastime, is extremely cruel. Imagine having a hook stuck into your mouth, being dragged by it and plunged into water until you died. The fish has a hook stuck in its mouth, is pulled from the water and left writhing on the ground until it dies.

There are other so-called sports which usually do not end in death, but do involve suffering – horse racing and greyhound racing, for example. If horses or dogs wish to race each other, fine! But the action has been turned into a business; people make a living, if possible a fortune from it, and so the animals are fine-tuned. What matters is victory! A tube may be inserted down a horse's throat so that it can draw in more air and run faster. This is using an animal as a machine. No wonder ailments include bone damage, bleeding lungs and an excessive heartbeat. During races, horses are whipped and forced to try and jump over very high fences; if they fall and are badly injured, they are, euphemistically, 'put down'.

Like horses, greyhounds may be run even when injured; there are fines for withdrawals and race meetings are rarely cancelled, even though rain may have made the course slippery. The bends on the track require the dogs to lean, and abnormal and repeated pressure is placed on their joints. Each year thousands of greyhounds are declared not good enough, and thousands are retired. The ones who do not have the luck to find a home face a harrowing death. There was a recent case of a man who made a living out of killing greyhounds.

Zoos can play a valuable role in protecting endangered species, then re-introducing them to their homeland, but where a zoo's real purpose is to enable humans to stare at creatures they would not normally see, as they once stared at deformed people in fairgrounds, they are cruel since they deprive the animal of its natural life for no reason other than human gratification. Plucked from their habitats, animals accustomed to roaming are imprisoned. How long does it take to explore a cage? I remember seeing a solitary bear in an enclosure. It looked utterly lethargic and dejected.

So should we not keep pets? Are they not also prisoners? Yes, they are, and I do not regard the keeping of fish and most small mammals as justified since they are unresponsive to human beings and, in general, they are not threatened with extinction. Let them go their own way. Cats, dogs and horses are another matter. They are not kept in cages. There is a two-way process. Given a decent home, they and their owners are happy. There is affection on both sides. Whether they would be happier still in the wild is impossible to say. If we gave them the choice they would stay. If we forced them out many would die, unable to fend for themselves; the remainder would form packs and, being large and ubiquitous, they would become a nuisance to man, who would hunt them. Over the centuries their lives and ours have become intertwined. Perhaps it is best to leave it that way.

For the entertainment of humans, circuses used to – and some may still – compel animals to perform unnatural acts. The trainers did not always rely on rewards of extra morsels, but also punishments of sticks, whips and electric prods.

In some parts of the world monkeys on chains and bears who 'dance' are displayed to tourists. The bears have had hot pokers pushed through their noses, followed by a rope; when the rope is pulled the bear writhes in agony. That is 'dancing'!

Given the principles proposed, if an animal is to be killed for food it should have, first, a long and contented life. To slaughter an infant because it tastes better is to trivialise and violate life. Chickens should not be crushed together in huts, never even seeing daylight. Sheep should not be crushed together in crates, and transported for hundreds of miles.

The killing itself should not be haphazard, as in shooting pheasants, nor indiscriminate, as in commercial fishing, nor prolonged, as in whaling – it should be sudden, immediate and virtually painless. There is, I understand, a Muslim ritual which insists that an animal is not stunned before its throat is cut. Any ritual that causes unnecessary fear and pain should be outlawed by the fundamental values of any religion.

Animal experimentation concerns life and death, but it is not a straightforward issue of humans or animals. We do not have to act against them for our survival; they are used for our benefit. The issue is between us and some form of affliction; we take treatment to try and overcome it. Animals don't have to enter the matter at all, but they are brought in as a safety measure – test the treatment on them first, and if it harms them don't use it on us. The experiments are to lessen risk, not to act out of necessity, and, therefore, they fall below the moral standard of only harming other life when it threatens us or when we need to eat it to keep ourselves alive.

If a person is facing death and only a certain treatment may save him, he may as well try it. Without it he will die, and with it he may live or die. The treatment is his only chance of life. An animal is irrelevant. If a person is not facing death, the situation is less serious and so it is less moral still to make some third party suffer because of it. Logically, in the case of death, and morally, in every case, it is wrong to experiment on animals. Yet in the UK millions of rodents and thousands of birds, dogs and primates are experimented upon each year, and in Europe thousands of mammals are used annually for the testing of cosmetics, such as skin creams and hair dyes.

Any treatment should be based on good reason for thinking it may be successful. There is a wealth of knowledge already, which should be fully accessed, and use should be made of mathematical models, and of human cells, tissue, blood and volunteers.

What works on other species may not work on humans. I have read that in Britain, over ten recent years, there was a five-fold increase in harmful reactions to drugs – drugs first passed as 'safe' on animals. So, practically, animal experimentation is far from foolproof, apart from being sometimes illogical and always immoral.

Without life we have nothing, which makes life more valuable than anything else. It is the fundamental right of each thing that possesses it. Therefore, unless we are in grave danger ourselves, don't destroy other life. So, don't pull up a weed. All life is essentially the same, so treat it the same. Therefore, if we do pull up a weed it is murder. We should be imprisoned or executed. Confronted by such conclusions, we soon set logic aside.

The ideal of not killing or hurting anything unnecessarily is repeatedly broken for reasons of safety, improvement, convenience, expense, time, comfort, sightliness, preference, taste and irritation or fear. It will be a long while, I think, before meat is never eaten and animals are not exploited, and gardens are not cultivated at the expense of the existing plants. Weeds are ever likely to be casualties.

Nature can be rampant and intrusive, and the case for destroying some of it, even though it is not imperative to do so, can be overwhelming. Will we not build houses and roads because of the vegetation and insects that will be harmed in the process? There are circumstances, and we reach a point where, though we may accept the sanctity of all life and we do not have to kill, it is just too much trouble not to, or not to act in a way which we know will probably result in death. Moreover, if nature flourished unchecked, there would come a time when it really did threaten our survival, and we would have to curb it, at the cost of more lives than are taken now.

Nonetheless, though the ideal may never be attained, like most ideals, it can be borne in mind, prompting us to justify causing a death or to draw back from it and thereby save a life. I do see growing respect for non-human beings. Vegetarianism is now commonplace. Animal welfare societies combat the cruelties I have outlined, and many more besides. Increasingly, people refrain from picking flowers; they plant trees, and apply chemicals that deter rather than destroy; they don't squash a fly shut in a room, but open a window; they prefer a dog harness to a collar, and a mousetrap which does not break the mouse's back, but imprisons it until it can be released away from the house. I do believe we are moving in the right direction.

If we value life and wish to reduce pain, we can save multitudes and avoid an enormous amount of suffering. Given that we will place ourselves first, that sometimes we will kill because the alternatives are impractical, and sometimes we will act with undue selfishness, still the ideal can be influential and indeed, on occasion after occasion, decisive. We only need to apply it more. We really can do better.

With the proviso of self-preservation, then, I propose an extended golden rule: let us treat other life as, if affairs were reversed, we would like other life to treat us.

FREEDOM, RESPONSIBILITY AND HAPPINESS

I have been prompted to consider how freedom relates to responsibility by working for people who live in hostels, on state benefits. They have been deemed incapable of employment, usually because of some impairment of their mental health, though for most of the time they come across as normal as anyone. In one hostel every occupant had his own room, heated and furnished. There were two lounges and shared bathroom facilities. Cleaners attended to each room, and one person to the laundry. Meals were provided. 'Key-workers' were on hand to deal with problems. Every day, residents could do as they pleased, within the law. What a lack of responsibility! What freedom!

Yet the amount of money these people received in benefits was small, so their choice of purchases and travel was very limited. After knocking, the staff could simply enter the rooms. They had keys. The hostel had rules such as the prohibition of alcohol, and when and where residents could meet guests within the building. Meals had set menus and set times – miss the time and they miss the meal. Key-workers were expected to meet with their clients regularly, learn details of their lives, and make and develop goals – which could be helpful, but is intrusive.

I began to wonder if, despite my obligations, such as working fixed hours most days of the week, I was not more free than the residents. It seemed, paradoxically, that without responsibility you lose freedom, for you become dependent upon the decisions of others.

The fact is, freedom comes in many forms, and being free in one way may entail being compelled in another. Taking on responsibility can lose some options, but gain others. We give up some freedom when we enter society and live under its laws, but then we become free from fear or, at least, as much fear. A wild animal roams where it will, but it is constantly in danger. I remember a scene from the film *Dr Zhivago* where a prisoner says to some people who are at liberty that he is free because he can speak his mind, and they dare not.

Fundamentally, freedom is about choice: the more choice we have, the more free we are, and we choose what we believe will make us happy. Happiness is the ultimate goal. It is the benchmark by which we judge the state of our lives. Different people achieve it in different ways, but it is the common aim.

To try and justify its status we can only point to its obvious, universal desirability, and to it being the most satisfying of feelings. Satisfaction, contentment, gladness, enjoyment – they are all ways of saying happiness. Its primacy is built into our feelings, thoughts and language. We ask somebody if they are happy. If they say no, we ask what's wrong; they should be happy, just as they should be well. If they say yes, that is sufficient – no doubt they could be happier still, but there is no state of mind beyond happiness.

Often, people seek the binding relationship of marriage. At work, they vie with each other for promotion. They deliberately increase their responsibility and reduce their freedom. But marriage brings companionship and security, and promotion brings more status and more pay. These gains make them happier.

Freedom and responsibility! We 'mix and match', aiming for the combination that is achievable and that makes each of us happiest. If we do choose responsibility, let us be free to choose it. Let us have as much freedom as we can with our own lives for no one has more justification for deciding how we spend our time on this earth than us; and the more choices available the more chance of doing what we really want to do.

There are, of course, physical constraints, and constraints we allow, or are virtually unavoidable, such as living within society. Life demands give and take. The boundaries, though, should be as few as possible, so that each individual can choose whatever gives him the most happiness.

EDUCATION

We learn about the world around us, and about ourselves. Every form of life learns – what is harmful, to avoid; what is beneficial, to embrace.

Humans have grown particularly sophisticated, and so has our way of life. No longer does a person exist more or less by himself, hunting for food, grunting for speech. We live in societies, communicate by words, buy articles with money, and obtain it by performing specialised jobs.

Words are written as well as spoken, then spelling and punctuation are useful. Money needs to be counted, and subtracted. Multiplication is helpful, and division virtually essential. So we come to the famous Three R's – reading, writing and arithmetic. Though, of course, it is possible to live without them, if we did we would either turn the clock back for all, or we would be very much in the minority, and find ourselves severely disadvantaged.

It is to everyone's benefit to learn the Three R's soon, and so education concentrates on the young, so much so that generally they are compelled to attend school from about the age of five. This is a gross deprivation of their liberty, but justified on the grounds that without it their futures would be very limited and poor in almost every sense, and they would be burdens on their modern society. They may grumble at the time, but, without education, they would grumble more later.

Starting at roughly five years old, many children are kept at school until they are about fifteen years old. It does not take ten years to learn the Three R's – they could be grasped after, say, three or four. But other subjects are taught as well, while English and maths become more complex.

Throughout our lives we learn, and at least some, and maybe much, of what we learn at school we would absorb later anyway. School, though, concentrates the mind and is a most constructive use of the time. It introduces subjects which may influence our choice of career, and interests which may enrich our lives. With full-time attendance, students should emerge into adulthood already competent and knowledgeable, to the benefit of themselves, employers and society.

If a child, knowing the basics, left school at about the age of eight, what would he do? Doing nothing in particular or some simple, repetitive job, assuming such work was available, would leave him less able to cope with a demanding job when he really did have to work, and less able to manage life in general since often he would come up against vocabulary, formulations and concepts he simply didn't understand. I think it best to insist on some education most days during childhood.

What should be taught? The world around us, and how to deal with it. We need to be able to communicate, and use money. The Three R's, therefore, are essential. The world itself could be introduced under that very name, an amalgamation of astronomy, geography, history and science. I have in mind factual statements about the solar system and the earth in particular, the locations and brief descriptions of countries, the naming of the oceans around them, an outline of man's past, and a simple account of the workings of the body and the nature of air and light. Such a syllabus would give a young child his bearings. I would also touch upon music, art and crafts and, more so, sport because of its contribution to fitness, and as a means of 'letting off steam'. The world would be taught, in its own right, from the start. There is no need to concentrate almost entirely upon the Three R's; they should be taught whenever they occur, whatever the context, by every teacher, if not every adult.

Moving to dealing with the world, useful skills would include how to prepare a meal, change a light bulb, a plug, a fuse and a washer, some car maintenance, and how to use a computer, which is particularly important since computers are now so much a part of everyday work and life. First-aid proficiency could be most beneficial.

From early days we are told that certain actions are right and others wrong. As we develop, therefore, the ideas of morality and society could be explored, and extended into some explanation of the legal system, and not only of basic laws, but other pertinent ones too, such as those concerning consumers and nuisances.

Some group makes the laws that control much of our lives, so it is relevant to learn about our political system, especially if we are expected to participate in it, as in democracy. Students could be taught how laws are passed and governments both national and local are formed, and of the populace's influence, such as in casting a vote. Our system could be compared with others, for assessment.

In considering morality, the law and political structures, concepts such as value, justice and rights would arise. We would be reflecting on the status of life. We do not have to consider also the purpose, if any, of life, but the question may well arise in discussion; beliefs of all kinds are a part of our knowledge of the world, and what to do with our lives is a question worth posing to young people who are about to set out on their own lives.

If they work, school leavers will pay income tax, and whenever they have purchased, they will have paid VAT. It would be useful to explain these and other taxes; also interest rates, credit and debit cards, insurance, mortgages and pensions.

Morality, beliefs, law, politics and economics! These subjects may seem more appropriate for universities than schools, but, with or without their titles, all are alluded to from an early age, and all could be taught during schooldays. Children have a keen sense of fairness, enabling them to appreciate the essentials of morality and the law. Each topic could be presented with a combination of facts and ideas. Some surprisingly profound discussion might ensue. The personal significance of the material would be clear.

So, I envisage the Three R's, 'the world', music, art and crafts, and sport occupying, roughly, the first half of school life; then pupils concentrating upon the new subjects described, plus some more traditional ones. A full list, therefore, would be skills, morality and beliefs, law, politics, economics, English, maths, science, history, geography, including some astronomy, a foreign language – reasonably the one most widely spoken apart from English – music, art, and sport – fourteen altogether; that could divide into each having at least two lessons a week, and some having three.

But I would create more space, and so allow more variation, by making music, art and sport optional extras at the secondary stage. Pupils would already have spent four or five years becoming acquainted with them, and so have a good idea of their nature and range. The next step in these three areas is not one of gaining more knowledge of general use, but of becoming a specialist, learning musical notes and playing an instrument, or creating artistic works or becoming proficient in some sport. Pupils do not need to go this far to know about the world; they can enjoy without being practitioners, so those who wish to perform should be prepared to learn privately, through tuition, societies and clubs. Therefore at a secondary level, music, art and sport should be taken out of the main curriculum.

I would not automatically fill the gaps with English and maths, only for those who were significantly behind in reading, writing and arithmetic. It is to be hoped most children would not need to catch up on the basics.

English, I emphasise, should be taught by everyone. Corrections should include grammatical as well as material errors.

Maths, like all subjects studied to a general standard, should concentrate on matters most people are likely to meet, and only glimpse what lies beyond for those who wish to venture there. I remember struggling with forms of algebra and geometry I have never, mercifully, met again.

Subjects interweave, so one lesson may well contain more than one subject. English is in everything. Maths is in science and economics. Skills are science in action. Morality, beliefs, law and politics draw on history and geography. We need to study English and maths directly, but not to be preoccupied by them. That should not be necessary. They make themselves felt naturally.

Every syllabus should be examined for its usefulness. Does it contribute to our understanding of the world, enabling us to participate in general conversation, form opinions and apply it professionally? Does it provide us with some of the abilities to cope with modern life? Does it point to ways of enriching our lives by introducing possible interests? Cut out, or mention only in passing, parts which most people are never likely to use. Watch out for too much detail – it will be forgotten.

For students not continuing into higher education, the final year at school could be spent in revision, examinations and work experience, not only of the work the individual thinks he would like to do, but, so far as is possible, of other types as well, so that he can appreciate more his choices. Such a year should help to reduce the restlessness which so often accompanies adolescence.

Some form of pupil assessment is important. Employers want a fair idea of a candidate's knowledge, ability and character. Society wants to know that education is achieving what it is meant to achieve, and, hopefully, the pupils themselves would like a measure of success.

Exams certainly test memory and some types of ability, including working under pressure, but the pressure is more than that encountered in everyday life, and the outcome is significantly, sometimes hugely, dependent upon sheer luck – topics and phrasing which the candidate has revised in particular.

Class work relieves the intensity and is likely to produce better work, but there is the opportunity to extract too much from others, resulting in the pupil appearing better than he really is. Confining class work strictly to the classroom and gathering books in at the end of each lesson still leaves the possibility of obtaining model answers between times, and bringing, perhaps smuggling, them into the next lesson.

Examination questions could be broad and there could be a wide and plentiful choice, so it would be highly likely that at least some of the matters revised would indeed come up. Examiners should ensure that they are not expecting too much in the time set. To allow for candidates' strengths and weaknesses, preferences and adjustments during the exam itself, the number of answers required could vary from a minimum to a maximum, with the marks divided accordingly.

Class work could include short exercises announced and completed within one lesson, rather like an exam, but with access to specific textbooks. Projects could be based on a definite collection of facts, pupils then having to arrange and express those facts themselves during the lessons. Of course, extracts could still be hidden, then copied, but hopefully a pupil will not always try to do this and whenever he does the system can only rely, as ever, on last-minute conscience, or detection, seeing or suspecting, by other pupils or by the teacher.

Over the lessons, over the years, through oral and written work, teachers should be able to form a good idea of a student's real standard, of his ability to grasp and solve problems, of his reasoning, imagination, vocabulary and inclination for particular subjects. They should also observe whether the student is cooperative, conscientious, considerate and polite. These traits are extremely important, at work and in society.

The views of various teachers, traditionally expressed in end-of-term reports, should be set alongside academic results. Such a practice would obviate the need for a reference, and be better than one since it would provide a few opinions and they, hopefully, would be honest rather than favourable.

For most of the time, the most effective arrangement for teaching is one to one. The teacher concentrates on the understanding of a single pupil, and the pupil can do little else but concentrate on the teacher. Unfortunately, however, such a combination cannot be afforded. So children are grouped together in classes.

Some educationalists advocate 'mixed ability' classes, deliberately placing the stronger with the weaker. The more able can work largely on their own, allowing the teacher to help the less able, while there will be occasions when they can all come together. The weaker may make a real contribution, and throughout, those who are slower are surrounded by a standard which, it is hoped, will encourage them to do their best and accelerate their development.

There is emphasis here on the less able child; the more able one seems to benefit only if his counterpart makes observations no one else has raised. It is likely that the stronger will be held back, and there is the danger that the weaker will not be stimulated but depressed as his own comparative shortcomings are laid bare day after day.

In practice, a topic will be explained, some pupils will comprehend and some not, and the class will break down into groups with the teacher trying to divide himself between them. The less able child will soon be left behind while the more able one will soon be left waiting, either for some explanation or more work. The differences grow with each lesson until the pupils can scarcely ever come together, and what we actually have is mini-classes, each of similar ability, within the one class. For everyone's sake it seems better to have outright 'similar ability' classes.

There will always be some variation in understanding, quality and quantity of work, and some waiting, but less if the students are roughly on the same level. Such an arrangement is less demanding on the teacher since he does not have to conduct several lessons in one lesson. Working among those who are about their own standard, students can develop naturally, with incentive coming – if not from personal motivation – from competing realistically with each other.

A child's ability, though, should never be cast in stone, as it were. There used to be an exam called the eleven-plus, since it was taken at the age of eleven. Those who passed were classed as able and moved on to grammar school; those who failed were not so able and moved on to secondary modern school, and, with rare exceptions, there they stayed, in their allotted places. But people are not that simple nor that predictable. They can develop, and decline, apply themselves, or not, have good and bad days, and show flair in some spheres if not others. So, there should be fluidity, and, to reduce disruption, fluidity within one school; each should encompass all ranges of ability, with pupils moving between classes depending on current strengths and weaknesses.

It is common practice for classes to split into sets – ability-based groupings – for certain subjects. I propose sets should be the classes in every subject; pupils placed appropriately at that time, with the opportunity to transfer at any time. A pupil could attend a different class in each subject.

There would be no need for a fixed, form class. A student could register his presence when he arrived at school, and be assigned to a teacher for pastoral care.

A teacher should know his subject. Keen to impart it to pupils, he tries to make it interesting, probably by a variety of methods – his own enthusiasm, and a combination of lecturing, discussing, questioning, viewing, writing, drawing, individual and group work, analysis of each other's work and visits to relevant places.

He should evaluate, honestly, his performance. What was good? What was bad? How can it be improved? Personally, I came to realise that I talked too much, and there was not enough variety in my lessons. The teacher's aim is to teach well.

For his part, a pupil should want to learn. Easier wished than realised! A child may not appreciate the worth of education, and regard school as boring and repressive. Energetic, perhaps noisy and showy, which impresses his peers, he may be more attracted to mischief than lessons, indeed, to causing mischief within the lessons. Goading the teacher is fun; learning what he is striving to pass on, isn't!

If pupils are disruptive, they need to be stopped. The usual line is reasoning and ordering. Then, if there is no improvement, a warning, and, if that too is ignored, punishment, such as extra work, withdrawal of privileges, suspension from school and, ultimately, expulsion. To these I would add measured, corporal punishment, as I would for adults. It could be an effective deterrent, and help to avoid the final step of exclusion and the problem of what to do with the miscreant then.

Attitude is fundamental. When a child starts school it should be made clear that he is to work with and not against the teacher, and the point should be reinforced as many times as is needed.

Whatever the ability, if a teacher wants to teach, and pupils want to learn, the lesson can be wonderful, full of pleasure and pride, all having truly, in the words of the cliché, fulfilled their potentials.

IMMIGRATION

The world is divided into different countries and usually we are the citizens of the country we were born into and grew up in. It includes our actual home, and we regard it, to some extent, as an extended home; we are familiar with its scenery, seasons and way of life, and we favour it, with a sense of patriotism.

Countries, though, interact, in alliances, trade, cultures and holidays, and sometimes members of one want to become – and sometimes they are invited to become – members of another.

A government's primary concern is with the citizens already in its borders, so before accepting any outsider it should ask, what will be his impact upon the native population? Factors to be considered include the sociability, skills and finances of the applicant, and the availability of housing and employment.

It would be unfair for an immigrant to immediately draw upon his new country's welfare system, or to be provided at once with council housing when there is already a waiting list. So he should have sufficient money to make a start, and reasonable prospects. Definite plans should be made, progress checked, and only when the candidate has established himself socially and economically should he be granted citizenship.

Among those trying to enter a country are asylum seekers; that is, people fleeing from their own land because it is dangerous to remain there. They may well arrive penniless and without any plans, but they are not immigrants at all. They are refugees and the humanitarian response is to provide refuge until the danger has passed and they can return. What if the problem persists? Then, if they wish to stay where they are, they can apply to become immigrants.

As soon as a refugee has recovered his strength and his wits he should be encouraged to work to pay for his keep. If he does not cooperate he risks being deported, and if he is prepared to face returning, I wonder why he left at all, and just how bad his situation in his own land really is.

To lessen economic strain on any one nation, refugees should be shared between nations. International cooperation is called for, and the members should apply pressure on a government that is making life for its citizens so unpleasant they want to leave.

An immigrant should try hard to fit into his new country. He has chosen it. His new country should try hard to fit him. It has accepted him. A newcomer does not want to completely abandon his traditions. Residents do not want their traditions seriously disrupted.

We all have our preferences in, for example, food, music, colours and appearance. Some people are inclined to be very house-proud, and some are not; some like to live in large families, and others do not. There are all types of personalities. We are quite accustomed to variety. When a person moves to another country, let him bring his lifestyle with him, providing it does not spoil the lifestyles of others. I have in mind intrusions such as a great deal of prolonged or repeated noise, unruly children or a householder allowing his property to deteriorate very badly and turning his garden into a junk yard; then, neighbours will quite reasonably object, and grow concerned about the valuations of their own properties. Potential house-buyers look carefully at a neighbourhood and often ask about those who live nearby.

Thinking back to the '50s and '60s one criticism of West Indians was loud music, and one criticism of Indians was strong, permeating cooking smells, and both were accused of over-crowding, resulting in more noise, more smells, more wear and tear and more rubbish. If somebody inflicts a bad experience upon us we are cautious about people who appear similar and so may inflict a similar experience. Moreover, the behaviour objected to may stem from popular, national traditions, associating it with the race as a whole, and so the race as a whole comes to be regarded suspiciously, leading to accusations of racial discrimination and, if the skin colour is different, of colour discrimination. The idea arises that one group rejects another simply because they don't like the look of them. In reality, some of the indigenous population are objecting to some of the activities of some of the new population, as they would object if these activities were carried on by anyone of any race, of any colour.

Another practice that can cause resentment is a concentration of foreigners in a small area. It is natural that people should gravitate towards others who are like-minded, and a person in a strange land will be particularly inclined to join those who share his origins, culture and language. He may indeed have arrived to live with his relatives – before living next door to them.

The native population, however, opens its doors to see a growing number of faces from abroad, unusual dress and mannerisms, shops which specialise in foreign items, religious buildings for other faiths and meeting places for other nationalities, and around are strange languages. They, the natives, may begin to feel as though they themselves are in another country. They may have a feeling of being taken over, and resent it. Then it is all the more important that the immigrants show a friendly face, demonstrate that though they are different in various ways they uphold the same fundamental social values, and can be as sociable as anyone.

Even so, there may remain natural citizens who dislike immigrants, or a particular race of them, for whatever reason. They may think the country cannot support them economically; they may be repelled by some of their habits or views, even though not anti-social; they may regard them as somewhat backward, making integration, at present, unfeasible; they may find their appearance simply distasteful; they may even have suffered at the hands of their countrymen, and any association raises bitter memories. Others can argue, drawing on data, urging tolerance and diversity, appreciating strengths and assisting weaknesses, pointing out the way we are, and making a distinction between 'some' and 'all'. One side may or may not convince the other.

Ultimately, anyone can like or dislike whatever he wants to. The mantra 'we are all the same' is reasonable in terms of human rights and in the application of the law. But the law should not bludgeon adults, and schools should not indoctrinate children into accepting that they must regard everybody in the same way. Their feelings and their opinions are their own affairs, which they should not be afraid to state.

Racism that consists of disliking people of another race may be seen as misguided, silly, even potentially harmful, but it is an individual's right, as it is to dislike anyone or anything. Racism that consists of actually harming, taking or damaging the possessions of, or harassing anybody of another race is a crime, as these acts are if committed against anybody of any race. If we really do not like something and we cannot change either it or ourselves, it seems best to have as little to do with it as we are able to.

A democratic government should consult its citizens. If the majority agree with immigration, the doors should be opened consistent with need and facilities. Everyone who approves should be welcoming and prepared for diversity; those who disapprove should not go beyond personal declaration and non-involvement.

The government itself and, given broad consent, many private companies will provide employment, but if any private employer does not wish to enrol a foreigner he should not be compelled to do so. It is for him to select who works for him among those who wish to work for him. It is his business.

Similarly, if the owner of a shop or a restaurant does not want to serve a foreigner, that too is his choice. A refusal may be unpopular, and cost custom; not employing someone may lose a good worker. But a person should be able to do as he likes with what is his, providing his action is not essentially criminal, just as a person should be able to do as he likes with his own patronage and his own labour.

There is emphasis on equal opportunities, and there is some practice of positive discrimination which in this case means appointing an immigrant to a job because that gives a sense of balance between races. Equal opportunities and positive discrimination are contradictory, while, in this context, the latter is also racial discrimination. For an employer, the obvious question is, who can do the job best?

Racial abuse, like racial discrimination in employment and services, is prohibited. Since the law is meant to apply to all, it must outlaw abuse aimed at any race, but the intention and the focus is to shield immigrants, especially from insults which centre on skin colour. This law brings the law into disrepute. The aim is to protect one section of society, which, thereby, favours it, contrary to the principle of equality; and the result is to declare that one derogatory remark – about race – is worse than another – about, say, parentage – which is quite subjective and contentious. It is also rather trivial. Other than a damaging lie, no insult is serious enough to be classed as a crime. We are all victims of name-calling from time to time. It is unpleasant, as is rudeness in general. But one-offs of this sort can be shrugged off. The law should become involved when abuse, in any form of words, is so persistent and troubling it amounts to harassment.

If a government feels that it needs to protect newcomers from its own nationals it should question its whole approach to immigration. Clearly, something is wrong and the intake should be stopped until the problem is resolved. Basically, the government should be moving with consent, not compulsion, and, having secured agreement on immigration in principle, it should also ensure the availability of housing and employment, and try to ensure the suitability of the immigrants. They, for their part, should have a good idea of the country they are planning to make their home, believe it is acceptable to them, and enter it in a spirit of friendliness. Goodwill, overall, on all sides, should lead to neighbourliness.

INCITEMENT

Incitement is a dangerous concept. It can be acted upon and cause harm; and it can also be used to suppress opinions. I start on the basis that we should be as free as possible, which includes freedom of speech. A person speaks words, and we agree or disagree with other words. If somebody tells lies they can be countered by the truth and, if they are damaging, the liar can be sued. A point of view can be met by other points of view. Words become dangerous only when they cause or are clearly about to cause serious harm, and against them are the words we have heard throughout our lives, that we should not harm.

Suppose somebody advocates and glorifies violence, perhaps in pursuit of some goal. Any normal person listening should know the fact that – and why – violence is not allowed, and peace is glorified, and, ordinarily the call will be dismissed out of hand. The authorities can ignore him. He is no real threat. There is no need to silence him. If his proposal is acted upon, the police act to stop the offence; if it is about to be acted upon, such is his impact, the police can demand that he stops, and they can caution his listeners. He himself may be placed under surveillance – not surprisingly, since his aim is to undermine the foundations of society. But unless and until he becomes a real danger, leave him alone. He has a right to speak his mind, however extreme, and others have the right to hear and make up their minds; some who hear may try to dissuade him, and may succeed.

It is likely that harming and damaging will not be suggested for their own sakes, but as answers to some particular grievance, and the people most influenced will be those who have the grievance. They should have the opportunity to present their case formally, for it to be thoroughly examined and a balanced judgement made. If the complainants remain dissatisfied, they may resort not to violence, but protest, perhaps through disobedience such as obstruction or non-payment of taxes.

These particular forms of protest, like violence, cannot be tolerated, for the first causes harassment and the second is unfair on everyone else who is paying the tax. The law covers all. So such actions, in their own ways, also amount to serious though not so blatant harm. Again, however, anyone proposing them should be free to have his say until he is on the point of causing such harm.

It might be asked, why allow somebody to start only to stop him if he becomes effective? Because the one effect that is not permissible is that of causing basic criminal action. Anyone has the right to question anything; such is debate, and out of it may grow reform. But a person does not have the right to interfere with the liberties of other people, or to opt out of his own responsibilities. What is stopped are not ideas, but lawlessness.

Suppose the authorities can't keep control and there is wide-spread disorder, even outright, bloody revolution. The first thing the victors are likely to do is re-impose the ground rules of society. We do not want to live in anarchy.

More common than calling for warfare or civil disobedience are opinions and feelings which collide with prevailing policies. Today there is emphasis on equality, not political or legal, which has long been recognised, but equality of difference, of our regard for other people, and their customs. We must not say one race or sex is better than another, and that is absolute. Beliefs and values are subjective. So we must not say one religion or lifestyle is better than another, only that we personally are following such-and-such a way of life, probably because that is how we have been brought up, but, of course, every other way is just as good. If we suggest something is better than something else we are criticising; with criticism comes dislike, which may incite hatred, which may cause crime. We want to live in harmony. Minorities, especially, need to be protected because they are vulnerable, so we should make a point of being complimentary to them – providing they do not disagree with an inclusive society.

Now to try and disentangle this mass of ideas! The fact that we are all of one species, all much the same, has led to the thought, enshrined as a principle, that we should be treated the same. So we all have rights and obligations. One right is to be able to air our own opinions; they are part of our personality, part of our lives, to be formed and, if we wish, expressed unless they seriously encroach upon other lives.

When we do not simply follow, but personally decide upon a certain opinion or view or way of life, we are implying we prefer it to other outlooks. We should be allowed to express our preference and state why we consider alternatives to be deficient.

Discussions may take place, and differences remain. Hopefully the sides can part on civil terms. Politeness is not essential, but it helps because it suggests a regard for others, and a wish to be cordial. Indifference, coldness and, of course, abuse are likely to prompt ill-feeling and retaliation.

Two people can agree to disagree and still exchange pleasantries. If feelings run so strongly and personally that they wish to have nothing more to do with each other, that, too, is their right. Society cannot, and should not try, to compel us to like one another. What it can insist upon is that we do not harm one another.

Some discord is a part of life. We are all likely, from time to time, to engage in cross words, and to be on the receiving end of insults and acts of rudeness. They come and go. The law should step in if they do not go; if their persistency makes our lives generally miserable. No one should be subjected to repeated abuse. Words can be hurtful, and if hurled often, and taken to heart, they amount to harassment, which should be a crime.

I have no wish to countenance name-calling or libel, or to poke fun at beliefs, but I have a definite wish to protect personal choices and points of view no matter how unpopular, indeed unsavoury, they may appear to many. So if somebody thinks that anarchy is better than society; that a crime – say, some forms of paedophilia or drug-taking – should not be a crime; that a certain lifestyle is morally wrong; that one sex is superior to another; that one race is superior to another, that it would be better for races to live apart; that for aesthetic reasons alone he does not like certain people; that as an employer or landlord he does not want to employ or house certain people; if anybody thinks or feels any of these things, he should not be howled or beaten down, convicted of intolerable discrimination, inciting hatred and not being 'politically correct'. He has an opinion, which is his right. To proclaim freedom of thought and to tell a person what to think is a contradiction.

I cringe when I hear people begin sentences with phrases like 'I know I shouldn't be saying this, but...' and I find repugnant cases of people being disciplined, indeed sacked, because they have expressed a sexist or racist or any other '-ist' point of view, let alone the law weighing in with fines and imprisonment. This is a characteristic of dictatorship! The stuff of brainwashing!

We all have personal likes and dislikes, thoughts and opinions, and preferences. We should be able to state them. Should somebody have a different outlook, so be it. To say that you dislike this or that is not in itself inciting hatred against it. You are declaring your choice.

It is incitement in a sense, that of urging, if a person tries to persuade others to hate something. There is, however, another sense of the word, the basic one of rousing or stirring up, and that necessitates considering the effect of what is said. That is the vital word – effect! Persuasion itself will not suffice for suppression, but the critical question is, are the words causing, or on the point of causing, basic anti-social acts, such as violence or harassment? The bar for incitement needs to be as high as this; anything lower is an infringement of freedom of speech; and at this height surely it can be included in the offence of 'disturbing the peace' – and so we can do away with incitement as a crime altogether, and so remove its threat to freedom.

I have considered the subject in general. I would like to add a few words relating it to the police in particular. Sometimes they themselves deliberately encourage crime: an example is police-women posing as prostitutes to entrap would-be customers. The justification offered is that ruses of this sort flush out criminals. They also incite criminality. Along somewhat similar lines, the authorities could set out a stall in the street, leave it apparently unattended but have guards hiding, ready to pounce on anyone who stole from it. Officers could disguise themselves as bank robbers and urge people to join the gang, or offer drugs for sale, ready to arrest those who tried to buy.

There may be an exceptional case for laying a trap to ensnare a specific criminal; as a rule, however, inciting crime is the very opposite of what the police should be doing. Certainly it is part of their duty to infiltrate, but not to instigate, not to be *agents provocateur*, deliberately leading citizens into temptation. They tell us we should do everything we can to prevent crime occurring at all. They would do well to heed their own advice: make safe and warn, not entice and arrest.

It appears to me there are more than enough criminals ready to act of their own accord, more than enough crimes to be solved and more than enough inmates in jails, without the police wilfully endeavouring to make more still.

SEX OR VIOLENCE

I am not considering these topics in real life where, of course, sex is allowed and violence is not, but in fictional life, in books, films and theatre, where acceptance is, rather, the other way round.

On the screen especially, violence is portrayed extremely graphically. Blows are shown in slow motion, people are tortured, disembowelled and decapitated, swords driven through their bodies and out the other side, limbs cut off with chainsaws, and acts of murder extended and extended until the victim, ferociously beaten, stabbed, shot, drowned and thrown off high buildings at last expires, perhaps.

I have vague memories of a film which began with a man being hit over the head with a shovel, and buried. That, surely, was the end of his life. Not at all! His hand pushed through the soil, he clawed his way to the surface and the murderer had to start all over again. The film – not a 'black' comedy – continued in similar vein – including a partial crucifixion, and, apparently, at some festival, won an award. The audience stood and applauded!

Not long ago another film was publicised as, 'the most violent film ever made.' That was a selling point. 'Unmissable!' the commentators raved. Audiences rave too! They enthusiastically describe, to those who have not yet had the pleasure of seeing, depictions of terror, agony and death. It is all quite acceptable.

Yet should a production, on paper, celluloid or stage, concentrate on sex as much as some concentrate on violence it is condemned as pornographic, and viewers as perverts.

I am not referring to works which imply – by innuendo, darkened scenes, suggestive poses and a few grunts and thrusts – sexual activity. These are just about mentionable, with an embarrassed grin, and trumpeted as meritorious in other ways. No, I have in mind works which show sexual parts and acts vividly, in detail and at length. Eugh!

So voyeurs, as people who like to look at sexual scenarios are now dubbed, keep very quiet, slinking in and out of 'private' shops, which must be faceless; or, finding it more bearable, have their wares sent by post, under plain cover, marked 'for the addressee only'.

But which is worse, violence or sex – drawn-out representations of excruciating pain and death or drawn-out representations of intense sexual intercourse? Morally, the answer seems plain enough. The viewers of violence enjoy watching others suffer; the viewers of sex enjoy watching others in ecstasy. Better to revel in pleasure than pain. Violence is bad; sex is not bad at all.

The fact that it is sexual and not violent material that is pushed undercover follows naturally from the fact that sex itself is pushed undercover.

Sex is, of course, a basic instinct. Most people desire it. Many people love it. Generally it is pleasant for all concerned. But it involves the genitals and proposes nudity, and through the ages both have been regarded as shameful. The genitals are also the outlets of excretion, a messy, smelly function which we want as little to do with as possible. So they repel. Yet they also attract. Many men like to look at naked women. Whether it is true the other way round I'm not so sure, but I have detected some interest, and I see that often women like to appeal to men while feigning disinterest bordering on dislike.

There can be few topics which raise as many contradictions, as much relish and revulsion, as sex. The upshot is that as excretion is kept within the closet, sex is kept within the bedroom. The acts are performed behind closed doors; the components are our 'private parts'; they, and what we do with them, are our business alone. We do not provide details. So be it. Fine! It is not details I am after, but more frankness and tolerance in our attitude to sex in general.

Men do like women, and women do like men, in a sexual sense. In truth, do you feel no pleasure in seeing beautiful bodies and imagining sexual acts? In public, however, we are conditioned to display indifference and, should the subject arise, distaste. We speak of others, not us. Ideas of privacy, embarrassment, rudeness and offensiveness, though weakened, still prevail, and are now reinforced by 'political correctness'. The buzz word is 'unacceptable', followed by 'discipline' and 'compensation.' Whatever we feel, we must say the right thing, act the right way.

So people who do show interest, who, indeed, look out for nudity and sex are not just odd, but, according to the social norm, disgusting. Really, they are acting naturally, and the revilers unnaturally in repressing their feelings – not that these feelings should erupt into some crime, such as rape; to that extent they must be tamed. But to deny or trivialise them is untrue and unnecessary.

Like the prudes, those who enjoy violence are also behaving unnaturally. Violence is a part of life. It is involved in the procuring of our food, in war, in some crime and in the suppressing of it, and in some punishment. We may be fascinated by the drama, we may enjoy the result, such as eating the food; we may gain satisfaction from seeing an act of justice performed, but to enjoy violence for its own sake is sadistic. To find entertaining in itself one living being inflicting pain upon another, whether in reality or in pretence, really is a perversion.

Sometimes sex and violence are combined. Some scenes include a degree of discomfort, even pain, portrayed as an aphrodisiac. Whatever the scenario, violence is the villain; not that I am calling for it to be banned in literature, films and theatre. It may be needed for the plot, and can be portrayed concisely and, to a large extent, indirectly.

The most important point: people should be free to see whatever they want to see, providing the participants are not coerced or duped. To force anybody of any interest into private shops, seedy cinemas and plain wrappers is too censorious. It is going too far.

I simply conclude, on the basis that sex involves happiness and violence unhappiness, that the first is good and the second is bad, and therefore it is people who are keen on violence, not sex, who should be met by looks and words of disapproval.

REACTING TO PAEDOPHILIA

The law decrees that a minor's knowledge of sex should be restricted to words, and it takes for granted that if a child agrees to a sexual liaison with an adult the child does not really know what he is doing – he is under the influence of the adult who should know better. Therefore paedophilia is proscribed as a crime, and the adult is prosecuted. I accept that it should be a crime, but I maintain that society's reaction to it has been an overreaction.

Reflecting on the past few decades I have noticed a growing concern for the welfare and happiness of children. Far from being 'seen and not heard', they have been encouraged to speak up and speak out. At school, lessons must be interesting, and they are often noisy. Teachers are not allowed to touch, let alone smack children; and parents too may soon be prohibited from smacking. If a child feels aggrieved there are helpers, face to face and on the phone. Anyone working with the young is now checked to see if they have a criminal past. The old injunction, 'Never take sweets from a stranger', has become the stark, blanket one: 'Say no to strangers'. Does emphasising importance and protection contribute to brazen behaviour?

When we regard something as particularly precious we are particularly vexed if anyone interferes with it. Paedophiles have drawn not just disdain, but outrage and loathing. It seems to me they have even brought about a new type of criminal sentence. I say, 'seems to me' because I am not a lawyer, but an interested observer, and as such I have noticed the apparent creation of a register – The Sex Offenders' Register.

Crimes and criminals have long been recorded, but if a person is placed on the register their movements and activities within the community are circumscribed, as if they are on parole. Yet people on parole have not finished their sentence, whereas people on the Sex Offenders' Register have, or at least had, according to custom and justice. Being registered is an additional punishment. I am not sure that this has been appreciated.

It used to be the case that if someone was sentenced to prison for a fixed period he was released at the end of it, and that was that. He had 'done his time'. The slate was wiped clean. He started afresh. Of course, he may still be stigmatised by some, but so far as the state was concerned he was a free man.

The fixed-term sentence itself took account of the nature of the victim. The vulnerable were recognised as such. An attack upon, or molestation of a child or a woman or an elderly or mentally handicapped person has long been regarded as worse than some sort of interference with an able-bodied man, and has resulted in a more severe sentence.

Sentences can consist of various components, say part prison and part supervision within the community, but each component must be less than the sentence itself; otherwise it is not a component, it is the sentence itself.

To make a criminal serve a standard term of imprisonment, whatever the tariff happens to be at the time, and afterwards to impose a curtailment of his liberties, be it for one day or for life, is two sentences – two punishments for one crime. That is clearly wrong.

Moreover, I am personally aware of a case where, although the registration was not for life, it may as well have been. I know of a man who was imprisoned for some sexual misdemeanour against children, then he was placed on the sex offenders' list, completed the period and for years, so far as I know, he has led and is still leading, an unblemished life. Recently he mentioned to someone that he had given sweets to a friend's children; the someone informed Social Services and they told the parents not to allow their children to have anything to do with him. The state seems to be saying that that man should have no further contact with children for the rest of his life. What of the fact he has already served two sentences? What of the possibility of reform? What of the concept of forgiveness? Should we all be punished for ever for a wrongdoing, or just murderers and paedophiles? Rare cases apart, the sex offender should be able to become an ex-offender.

It is often claimed that even after their sentence has finished, paedophiles need to be watched because they are likely to strike again. Are they more likely to reoffend than, say, thieves or people who are inclined to violence? Prisons contain recidivists of all sorts. Perhaps, then, if only the manpower permitted, every ex-prisoner should be supervised, but unless that was for twenty-four hours a day, as in prison, there would be the opportunity to reoffend.

Knowing where an ex-criminal lives would enable the police to question him soon should a crime similar to the one he committed occur in the neighbourhood. The crime would have to be very similar indeed, though, or questioning him at all, for no other reason than for an offence of the same classification, would be unwarranted. Also, a visit from the police could threaten his attempt to lead a normal life, depressing him and raising the suspicions of those around.

Supervision could allow someone to judge if an offender is likely to strike again, and if they thought that he was, they could tighten the curbs, and compel him to attend some kind of course of counselling or rehabilitation. These measures might help – though the obvious time for courses is within prison. Super-vision, however, would need to be built into the sentence, a part with other parts accordingly smaller; it would amount to the offender being released on parole.

Checking on anyone whose sentence has finished is unjust. They are free to start again. If they commit more crime, they are arrested and punished again. That is justice!

At times paedophilia is described as an illness. Those who are afflicted can't help it. Then they should be pitied and treated. If confined at all, they should be in a hospital, not a prison. As it is, they are commonly damned as both bad and mad. Any derogatory word will do.

Ex-paedophiles striving to resume a life in the community are subjected to abuse, graffiti, damaged property, assault and, occasionally, murder. The devils who commit these crimes do so in the name of righteousness!

Within prison some convicts are separated from others for their own safety. These include sex offenders. Thugs who will readily bludgeon a victim into a vegetative stupor decide that a person who has sexually molested a child deserves to be tormented in every way imaginable – inserting razor blades in his food, for example.

What has brought about such blind and unremitting hatred? I suppose, for the public in general, it is the combination of children and sex; images of wide-eyed innocence, helplessness and obscenities.

Let's try to be calm, honest and factual: the law treats, or should treat, each case as it is. In our society, if someone murders a child he is punished by a life sentence; if he rapes or tortures a child he may well receive the same or at least a heavy sentence. As with all crime, the more harm, the more punishment.

Paedophiles who murder, rape or torture are, thankfully, very much the exception. Far more common are those who try to induce children to undress, and look at or touch and fiddle with their genitals. The basic instincts are those of attraction and sexual desire; instincts, remember, shared by all of us. We like, and desire, beauty. Before reacting with anger, it is worth looking, really looking, at ourselves. But we are expected to, and may well want to, observe boundaries and practise self-control. Some of us slip and are punished.

There may be no physical injury caused by a paedophile who mildly interferes with a child. Attention, though, is also drawn to possible mental harm. If a child is really aware of what is happening, it may be a distressing, even traumatic, experience. I say 'possible', and 'maybe'. My own teenage years were spent in a male boarding school. Various sexual shenanigans went on. Boys agreed or were persuaded, even intimidated, but whether they found their experiences playful or disgusting, I do not recall anyone becoming traumatised.

Suppose, however, someone is so shocked that there are changes in their personality. Again, for many years, I sense, the law has included this factor in the balance. If say, a robber beats a person with the result that apart from physical injury, the victim becomes timid and anxious, fearful to answer his door or to leave his home, then these consequences are, or should be, reflected in the sentence. Similarly, if a child is so affected by a paedophiliac experience that his outlook and behaviour are damaged, the greater the sentence.

Generally, during our lives, we all encounter some distressing events – rejections and losses, for example – and as time goes by they become less distressing. We adjust. We don't forget, but we recover. This natural improvement should also be considered.

To wring out every last drop of justice, sentences could be reviewed at fixed intervals and, depending on the current situation, increased or decreased accordingly. This, however, could be impractical, clogging up the courts, and disruptive, affecting lives which had become settled. All in all it is probably better to continue with one final sentence using observation, case histories, reasonable generalisations, such as the more the harm, the longer to recover, and approximate calculations, such as financial ones.

Some adults claim they were abused as children but did not report it, perhaps because they were afraid or embarrassed, or thought they would not be believed, or that reporting it would be disloyal to friends or family, but they are ready to speak out now. Society is more sympathetic now. So be it. Still, however, they need to be closely questioned about their reason for not complaining at the time. Were their reservations not to tell what they knew to be wrong really that great? If so, why wait as long as twenty or more years before making a charge? The court would have to be satisfied that the claimant was not really acting maliciously or to gain financially, and, of course, the evidence, now far in the past, would have to suggest, strongly, that the accused was guilty.

I do not seek to defend paedophilia, but to place it in perspective. I hold that because it is at least potentially harmful to those who need protecting it should be classed as a crime; that in most cases paedophiles are responsible for their actions and, therefore, they should be prosecuted and punished. But it needs to be remembered that most paedophiles are not sadists and murderers, and what they do should be compared to what other criminals do. Playing with private parts is not as evidently damaging as drawing blood and breaking bones. The vulnerability of the victim, and any shock, should be reflected in the one commensurate punishment, bearing in mind that sooner or later people generally recover from shock. The paedophile should be allowed to serve his sentence in the same way as any other criminal, and having served it he should be able to get on with his life in the same way as any other citizen.

Some years ago, during a robbery, a man had petrol poured over his trousers, around his genitals, and he was told that if he did not disclose some information the petrol would be set alight. A paedophile, for his part, commonly fiddles with genitals. Supposing the robber had acted on his threat, who would have done the most obvious damage? Clearly the robber. Who would be regarded as the worse criminal? I suspect, the paedophile.

Terrorism

Terrorism can have two faces. Often terrorists can be seen as criminals, especially, of course, by the authorities, or as freedom fighters by those who believe they are battling against some injustice, such as a repressive government or a particular policy, or to obtain some land which they claim really should be theirs. Today's terrorists can be tomorrow's heroes. Perhaps nobody exemplifies this better than Nelson Mandela, guerrilla leader, then living martyr and, finally, statesman feted all over the world.

The most widespread terrorism at the moment is that carried on by Muslim extremists. Their motives seem to be to drive foreign influence out of predominantly Muslim countries; carry out sabotage within the offenders' own countries as part of that aim and as punishment for wrongs past and present; a hatred of the Western way of life, which they consider sinful; and a wish to destroy and replace it with their own way of life.

I would like to think that conquest for the sake of grandeur is buried in history, but I hope there will always be nations prepared to intervene if a government is killing, or cannot prevent the killing of, its own people. It is an utterly shameful fact that sometimes the United Nations – the policeman of the world – is prevented from acting because some of its members rank trade before life; and at times some members are hypocritical, paying lip service while drawing back from committing their own troops.

Whatever the real reason for the 2003 invasion of Iraq, a laudable reason was to topple a tyrant; similarly, in Afghanistan it was right to oust the Taliban because of the hideous existence they had imposed upon its people. Given fundamental feelings and values, brutality should be opposed unconditionally. It justifies military intervention. Life should be saved and suffering ended.

Accepting that our lives are ours and so ours to do with as we wish, so long as we do not damage those of others, then we should have as much choice and personal control as possible, and the only political system which provides these rights is democracy. Therefore dictatorships should be opposed – though, if benign, not militarily – unless the citizens have actually and freely voted for them.

Muslims who object to intervention in their country should ask, firstly, is it there to protect from chronic deprivations, starvation, unjust imprisonment, torture and murder? If so, good! Muslims who object to Western intervention in particular should examine why, exactly, they dislike the West. Is it because of something in the past? Sooner or later the past can only be put behind us. Is it because they disagree with Western beliefs and lifestyles? They should understand that people can feel as passionately about freedom as they do about what is important to them; and variety in beliefs, customs, policies and aesthetics is an expression of freedom. We should be able to disagree and still live together.

Oppression can be a reason for terrorism, but oppression should not occur in a democracy, nor in its foreign policy. Within the country itself there should be equality, and any troops it has in another country should be there for extreme, humanitarian purposes. Trade implies influence, but trade should be advantageous all-round.

To hate us suggests an historical grievance which cannot now be undone, or fanatical opposition to our principles and practices. Kill us or turn us into Muslims! But we do not wish to become Muslims, and any attempt to force us is, according to our own precious values, totally wrong and naturally, it will be resisted.

How do we resist? By treating these terrorists as criminals, and not as freedom fighters. Clearly they do not have our freedom, but our enslavement at heart. They see themselves as warriors, but they do not fight on a battlefield. The war in Iraq was a success. Saddam Hussein's army was swept aside; his despotism ended. What followed, from time to time, was that individuals sneaked up, fired a shot or planted a bomb and melted away, literally in the case of suicide bombers. Realistically, these acts of violence can never be stopped. So long as there are people, crime can never be eradicated. Somebody can always hurt somebody else; in doing so, he is not winning a war, and we should not despair; he is committing a crime and we should try to bring him to justice.

To murder some members of the public by, for example, blowing up a train, is as futile as it is wicked. It will not change a society nor a foreign policy. Nonetheless, terrorists strive to carry out such atrocities, and we must strive to thwart them by being vigilant and reporting suspicions.

The authorities must perform their duty, at home and abroad; incorruptible, fair, and just with any crimes committed by their own forces. Troops that are in another country should demonstrate that they have the population's welfare at heart; then citizens should not wish to give succour to wreckers, but to help drive them underground and into oblivion. If the community has divisions it needs to avoid what its enemies would love to create – civil war.

I appreciate this is easier said than done, that there may be some anger about occupation and some sympathy for those taking up arms against it. But when terrorists viciously intimidate the people, use them as shields and present them with an enclosed life; and when, on the other hand, civilised forces try to establish order, restore the economy and offer choice, I trust the people see where their interests lie, and support accordingly. Together we can only make it as difficult as possible for terrorists to hurt us – and encourage everyone to place life before death.

Monarchy

Often, among animals, one dominates. He is the strongest; he wants the best; others fear and obey him. Such are the origins of monarchy. Using brains as well as brawn, a human animal gains power. The people become his people; the country, his country. He demands the tastiest food, the most beautiful women, fine raiments bedecked with jewels, enormous, ornate palaces and statues with plinths proclaiming his magnificence. To be hailed as really great he needs an empire, so he declares war on any nation he thinks he can defeat and despatches his subjects to fight and die for him.

He gives himself a title – King, Pharaoh, Caesar, Emperor – and sometimes he claims to be no less than a god waiting for his assumption to recline among other gods. Come the day, his decorated body is most venerably placed in a palatial – what else? – mausoleum his people have spent their lives building for him. Who dare do ought but quake, bow and serve?

Monarchy, however, collided with democracy, which gives worth to the lives, rights and opinions of each and every one of us, and over the centuries democracy has prevailed. Nowadays, dictators, royal or otherwise, are reviled.

Occasionally, royal families have been wiped out. More often they have surrendered some authority, become known as constitutional monarchs which, we are invited to believe, somehow reconciles them with democratic principles, and generally softened their image to suggest that really they are just one of us.

In Britain, in particular, monarchy was abolished but restored, and now the king or queen resides mainly in a palace in the capital city, and otherwise in castles, mansions and estates situated all over the country. Indeed, some members of the royal family have titles added to their names attaching whole areas of the country to themselves – the Prince of Wales, for example.

Not surprisingly, the royals are very, very rich and made more so, by the millions, by taxpayers, and for what? For ceremony! We do not need a professional dinner host, ribbon-cutter, bottle-breaker or reader of what the government says it will do. Ships can be launched, and roads and bridges opened by those who have actually built them.

The monarch is presented as a figurehead, a personification of the nation, so to oppose monarchy is to oppose the nation. These ideas should be disentangled. It is natural to feel affinity for the country where we are born and grow up, and to support it. No monarch is needed to instil or reinforce this inclination. There is an old slogan, 'For king and country.' It is quite reasonable to be against king and for country. There seems to be no shortage of patriotism in America, and if the president is likened to a king, officially he is a politician subject to the ballot box. Similarly, we have a prime minister.

The royal family is also presented as the embodiment of 'the family', a model example to which we can all aspire! Considering its actual conduct, is it such an example? Anything regarded as exemplary is scrutinised particularly closely, and criticised particularly heavily should it fall short of the ideal. Perhaps there are families around the corner that embody the characteristics of family life better than the royals, and without payment.

To retain royalty because it is part of our heritage is a very wasteful exception to the usual practice of preserving our heritage in books and museums. Enthusiasts who wish to keep the past alive can, of course, play the part from time to time; so anyone can, if they wish, impersonate some bygone king or queen. But to maintain the real thing, day after day, because our ancestors used to have it is as absurd as maintaining lords of the manor because our ancestors used to have them. Consign royalty to history!

Such constitutional functions as the monarch still holds can easily be removed, without ill effect. We can forego royal assent to laws, and whatever protection the king or queen is meant to afford the Church of England. If there is a parliamentary crisis, Parliament – and, perhaps, even, the people – can resolve it. In any case, the monarch is intended to act on the advice of his ministers.

The whole notion of a privileged family expecting others to be obsequious jars in a democratic society. Monarchy can be reconciled with democracy only by people voting in its favour. In Britain, as with almost everything, they have never been asked; if they were, most might say 'yes', perhaps out of sentiment, but not out of practicality. There is simply nothing worthwhile for a monarch to do except return his wealth to the people.

It is enough to make a beggar choke on his chicken – if he had any – to be told, as he shivers in a doorway, that his king, recumbent on a sofa, wishes him a happy Christmas. The British royal family smiles benevolently, dabbles in charity and allows into its presence people who are truly good, while taking for granted a standard of luxury almost unimaginable to those it is meant to care for, and a standard it is determined to cling on to. But any usefulness the role ever had has long since gone.

The royals should have gone with it, and should go now. Nothing drastic! I do not call for the guillotine. But they should be ordered to pack their bags – with not too much household silver – and leave behind the national assets for the benefit of the nation.

WHAT IS PHILOSOPHY?

To the popular mind, philosophy is concerned with generalisations about the nature and purpose of life. It immerses itself in the fundamentals of religion, morality and politics. It goes beyond observation and explanation to meaning. Philosophy wrestles with questions such as what really matters? How should we live? What is the point of life? Philosophers are expected to offer answers.

To the modern, academic mind, philosophy is concerned with the nature of knowledge. What do we really know, rather than what we think or believe? All factual statements can be doubted. There might have been a mistake. All sentences built around the verbs 'should' or 'ought' are value statements. Values vary; they are subjective, opinions, and, therefore, contentious.

So do not start with what we know, but what we assume, and draw strictly logical deductions from the assumptions. It is the deductions that are knowledge. 'It is raining', for example, implies drops of water, which are descending, and wetness; it does not imply dullness, or dislike or raincoats – these are ideas commonly associated with rain, but not necessary consequences of the word.

Ensure that the logic is undeniable – do not overstep the steps – and do not contradict yourself. You cannot maintain that something is both so and not so without reducing your statements to nothing. These are the answers offered.

For the population, philosophy is about life; for the professional it is about logic.

In the late 1960s I attended a lecture by the well-known philosopher A J Ayre called 'The Nature of Philosophical Enquiry'. He claimed that philosophy is not about interpreting the world. It has no special subject matter. It is 'to help clarification'. I think he said, with typical plainness, that it 'helps us think straight'. It is not useless – otherwise he wouldn't be doing it. Given a problem, the role of the philosopher is to identify exactly what the problem is, and the correct ways of solving it.

On this analysis, the aspiring philosopher should study scepticism and assumptions, meanings and senses of words, and logic. He should look at the works of traditional so-called philosophers only in so far as they discuss the nature of knowledge, ignoring their discourses on the nature of man, ethics, politics, theology and life in general. Having assimilated possibilities and procedure, the modern philosopher should be ready to identify the nature, and means of solving, any problem from, say, a stain in a carpet to world poverty, though he would leave the details and the treatment to the experts.

So, confronted by a stain in a carpet, he would make many assumptions about the existence of all the components, then he might accept the relationship of causation, rather than just a succession of events, and ascertain what caused the stain or, more precisely, what it actually consisted of; thereby, assuming the aim was to remove it, the experts could apply the correct chemicals and materials and in the correct proportions, which they would decide. The philosopher might offer advice, such as not to walk on the carpet while it is wet, not that this follows from the removal of the stain, but it is likely that we do not wish to replace one blemish with another one.

When in doubt about the meaning of a word, turn to a dictionary. The word 'philosophy' means, basically, 'love of wisdom'. What is wisdom? It is not about acquiring knowledge, but applying it, and it is possible for information to be gained from experience alone. Some people who neither read nor write are described as wise. They have absorbed the workings of the world around them, seen how circumstances unfold, the constancies and the variations, and they offer advice, in particular and in general. People who can read can add the experiences of those they have never met, or been told about.

I think of wisdom as balancing various considerations. So philosophy is appreciation of this process and conclusion. But what is the subject content? None is specified. We can be wise about anything. Philosophy can be seen in practice, but not on any matter in particular. Its traditional components – ethics, theology, politics, logic – fall away.

As a noun, philosophy is bound up with wisdom. As an adjective, philosophical, it often describes the states of acceptance and calmness, especially in the context of misfortune – someone who is sanguine in the face of adversity can be described as philosophical; or, someone who has good fortune, but appreciates that it can be lost in an instant can also be called philosophical; they know that life is full of 'ups and downs'. There that word – life – again, and a generalisation about it!

Wisdom consists of reflecting on events and actions, and drawing conclusions which are offered as guidelines. In the past philosophy has practised this on a grand scale, considering not the nature of stains, but the nature of man and of existence. It has included all branches of knowledge. Some of these, such as the sciences, have become specialised, though philosophers may still use them.

In the popular understanding, philosophy is, and always has been, concerned with the great questions, the why and how of life, and to try and answer them it considers theism, science, behaviour, values and political systems.

Common usage defines a word. What dictionary could not take into account homosexuality as well as happiness in explaining the word 'gay'? And this has been a recent innovation. Philosophy's components have been accepted for thousands of years. It is not just the sum of two words, 'love' and 'wisdom'. People have given it definite subject-content, summarised as the nature, conduct and purpose, if any, of life.

Better, perhaps, that some philosophers go with the flow rather than whittle their subject to nothing, and, if they are to be consistent, declare themselves to be redundant.

DOUBT AND KNOWLEDGE

There is a story that the philosopher Rene Descartes considered what he knew without any doubt whatsoever, and he concluded that all he knew was that he was thinking – therefore he existed. Unfortunately he was not justified in presuming an 'I'. All he knew was that some thinking was happening – therefore thinking existed.

When I was a student, René Descartes marked the beginning of modern philosophy, which was characterised by cutting off its traditional parts while studying the philosophies that taught them, and clinging only to tautologies, such as A is the same as A, and syllogisms, such as 'Grass is green, this is grass, therefore this is green'. Of course, all grass is not green. But the only philosophical error was contradiction. Statements, rather than suppositions, were subjective, and so did not count as knowledge.

I remember considering the meaning of the word 'same'. An A, for example, cannot be the same as another A. By writing 'another' I have implied they are separate, which is further implied by the word 'they'. One is spoken later than the other; one is written on a different portion of paper to the other. A thing can only be the same as itself. So, it seems, even tautologies fail as knowledge, though I think they can be redeemed with refinement.

We can say A means the same as A, and then consider what we mean by the word 'mean' – something along the lines of 'amounts to' or 'has the same worth as'. We are trying to say that fundamentally they are the same, though literally they cannot be; that they have the same significance but not place in space and time and, perhaps, not quite the same form: that repetition does not alter essence – that A is essentially the same as A, and not the same as B. This example illustrates the problems that can arise if we pursue the meaning of a word; and it also illustrates that the exercise can become unnecessary, impractical and obscure.

Some words or statements can be true in one sense but not in another, so the truth depends on the sense intended. The word 'good', for example, demands a setting; and if we say something is successful it is likely that it is successful in one respect, but not in another. We can debate the strength of words, the difference between, say, 'dislike' and 'hate'.

Sentences can be too simple or too complex, imprecise, unclear or muddled. Our uses of words have their failings, our constructions of them can always be improved. But everyday a colossal number of sentences are spoken which are quite clear. They are understood and responded to, without dissection. We are not usually left asking, 'What do you mean?' There is no need for doubt. The statements pass as knowledge.

Sense experience is an easy prey for the sceptics. They can always say perhaps we did not really see or hear or touch or smell or taste what we thought we did. Perhaps we were mistaken. If so, there remains the thought itself – unless it is claimed that also was mistaken. But why should there be doubt at all?

We are born with sense perception. It acquaints us with the world. It provides us with raw material which appears as much the same to all, or nearly all, of us. If two people look at, say, a tree their descriptions are likely to be very similar, as one would expect. If one person did not sense what everyone else did, we would conclude that person was in some way physically deficient and look for a medical explanation – unless it could be shown that the 'everyone else' was at fault, or even being malicious. Unlike, say, an election, sense experience is not decided by the majority. It is more than an opinion. It is not a reasoned judgement. What we sense strikes us, without thought, as external and blatantly immediate, vivid and evident. It warrants the description 'factual'.

Given the same machinery, as it were, and honest intent, we anticipate the same result, and what we all – or almost all – sense we can say we know unless there is actual, rather than imaginary, reason for thinking otherwise.

Moreover, if one person who, we assume, has normal senses, reports that he has sensed something, that too we can accept as knowledge, providing we do not have a factual basis for doubting it.

Strict deduction will always be certain – if we say the words expressing it are not really what they seem to be, still the thoughts conveyed by the words lead to an inevitable conclusion. Sense experience will always be open to questions, but if the questions themselves are not grounded on sense experience they remain no more than thoughts, no more than mental constructions which make no impact whatsoever on the original assertion.

Possibilities are concerned with 'might', sense experience with 'is', and, logically, we cannot move from 'might' to 'is' without 'might' becoming 'is'.

Many possibilities are inherently improbable to the point of silliness. Suppose someone said he saw a tree and somebody else claimed that person did not really see a tree, but a telephone box. It's possible! I suggest our initial reaction would be that a person acquainted with both would know the difference. If the sceptic persisted, we could check the spot ourselves, or we could ask is there a reason why a tree should not be there? Is the observer lying? Is his sight impaired? Was the light bad? If the answer to these queries is no, and likewise to any similar questions, we can accept that he saw a tree because there is no reason to think that he didn't.

For devilment, an individual may respond to all statements with the phrase, 'prove it!' We have proof, in logic and in the world. So while it is true that one kind of knowledge is more definite than another, it is contrary to language and custom to rule that the other is not knowledge at all.

If truth was restricted to deductions from assumptions we would be left repeating an exercise beginning with 'if'. We would know one thing – that words can be so arranged that they necessarily imply a conclusion. As it is, we know billions of things. Our senses and reasoning supply them. If anyone doubts it, let him supply not just a possibility – perhaps a quite unrealistic one – but a real reason. No reason, no doubt!

'IS' AND 'SHOULD'

I remember, at university, an academic asking me, 'How do you deduce 'should' from 'is'?' I muttered something which drew no more than an 'umph!' He didn't know the answer and, it seemed, nor did I.

The usual distinction between 'is' and 'should' is that 'is' describes matters of fact, such as, 'John is sitting down'; 'should' describes matters of value, such as 'John should be working'. The first statement is based on an observation, common to all with normal eyesight; the second is a judgement, and judgements may vary from person to person. The statements are of different types.

'Deduce' implies logical necessity; given a certain premise there must follow a certain conclusion. Mathematics comes to mind: two plus two must equal four. There is also the syllogism – one I often heard was, 'All Russians play chess. Ivan is a Russian. Therefore Ivan plays chess'. The fact that all Russians do not play chess is irrelevant in the present context. We are concerned with words and their relationships to each other. Given the first two statements, the third must follow. A factual syllogism would be, 'All men are mortal. John is a man. Therefore John is mortal.'

The usual teaching is that since 'is' and 'should' express different kinds of statements, the first, factual, the second, prescriptive, we cannot, strictly speaking, deduce one from the other. We can say that given a certain set of circumstances, it is good sense to follow a certain course of action, that it would be strange not to act accordingly, but that is not a strictly logical deduction. It does not follow that if we did not act in that way we would be contradicting ourselves, and that is what makes logical necessity, that not to draw the conclusion is not just wrong, it is a contradiction.

One may attempt to argue that all statements are essentially of the same type. There is no real distinction between 'is' and 'should'. They are both subjective. What I sense is my personal sensation; it cannot be anybody else's. But, in fact, what I see, hear, touch, smell or taste is essentially what everybody else does, to the point that if anybody did not sense the same that person's sensory system would be at fault; whereas, not our recognition, but our evaluation of what we sense, is entirely a matter of opinion. Unless we were physically impaired we would all see, and describe in a similar way, for example, a chair; whether or not the chair should be, say, painted would be a question which drew a variety of answers, according to personal preference, and there would be no obvious and universal criteria for deciding it. It would remain open, a point of view.

Basically, factual statements describe what is received by one or more of the senses; value statements are a reflection upon what is received by one or more of the senses. The truth of the first is measured against the sensations of others; the second has no common truth – individuals have different likes and dislikes, values and priorities, and make different judgements.

So even when 'is' and 'should' are analysed to their roots they are not the same – with one exception. There is a sense in which they, and 'must', do mean the same, the sense of correctness. We can say two plus two is four or should be four or must be four, meaning that any other answer is incorrect. Another example would be water is wet or should be wet or must be wet, or else it is not water. Wetness is a necessary characteristic of water. It is part of the definition. In such examples, however, 'should' is not being used as a word of value, but of logic. The conclusion, or description, is built into the premise or subject. It follows necessarily. But an opinion is not built into a fact, or can it be? Our problem is, how to deduce, by pure logic, a course of action from what our senses present to us as a fact.

I have been thinking about the proposition 'John is hungry. There is no reason why he should not eat. Therefore he should eat.' The second sentence takes away all objections to John eating. He is hungry – which, presumably, he does not like. There is nothing to stop him ending that condition. Nonetheless, however odd it may seem if he did not end it, it does not follow necessarily that he should. The point is, no conclusion is compelled by sheer logical deduction from the statements about 'hungry' and 'no reason', so that if we did not draw a conclusion we would be no less than contradicting those statements.

I have to accept facts cannot necessarily imply opinions, only other facts, and opinions only other opinions. They are, indeed, different types of statements.

Yet, if John is hungry, he wants to eat, and there is no reason why he should not, it is entirely logical that he should. There are many situations consisting of circumstances and desires where nothing follows necessarily, but one thing follows rationally. If a person is hungry, eat; if a car is to move, start the engine; if a piece of string is too long, cut it; if there are not enough chairs in one room, borrow one from another. Time after time, a next step is called for, and the next step is logical, and not just logical, but also obvious. How often do we hear people say such and such a solution is obvious?

It is not implied necessarily. In strictly deductive terms, we have a set of statements, some of inclination, some of observation, and no conclusion is compelled. We can construct sentences that really do necessitate a conclusion – for example, a hungry person should eat; John is hungry; therefore, it must follow, he should eat. But the premise itself is contestable. It has force only as part of the syllogism, not because it is blatantly or undeniably true. We might not accept it. A hungry person might be fasting, so he should not eat. So long as we are not denying what our senses clearly tell us, and not maintaining both 'should' and 'should not', then no contradiction is involved if we reject the proposition.

In practical terms too there are probably always alternatives to the one that presents itself. A hungry person could be fed intravenously; a car could be pushed; a piece of string could be doubled over, and a person could sit on the floor. But these solutions are roundabout, or, in the case of the last one, uncomfortable, and probably undesirable, and it is illogical to use a method with drawbacks when there is no reason not to use one without drawbacks.

There will be occasions when the next step is debatable. But frequently one course of action will stand out, logically, above all others, and wishing to give it a title I will call it not a logical necessity, which it is not, but a logical priority.

FREE WILL AND COMPULSION

By 'free will' I mean, basically, that the individual decides for himself; by 'compulsion' I mean that somebody or something decides for him. I think that compulsion is a word more commonly used and understood than determinism, and I say 'basically' because for a complete expression of free will there must be the chance to act upon the decision. If a person is sentenced to prison, and decides not to go, he will be taken there anyway. His free will exists only in a mental sense; in practice it is nullified. Force negates free will.

I make a distinction between 'wishing' and 'deciding'. A person may wish to eat a piece of cake, but decide against it because, for example, he is on a diet. He is deciding against his wishes, but he is exercising free will.

Then there is the power of influence. Sometimes people say, or we infer, that they believe in a certain religion, dress in a particular way and practice various customs because that is how they have been brought up. We have all been influenced by the societies in which we live. But as we develop our own personalities we may change our views and practices. I daresay we know of cases – perhaps we ourselves – of people who have done so. Clearly we have the ability to change. It may be difficult, it may incur disapproval, but we have the free will to do it. Many of us insist on being able to make up our own minds.

The subject grows more subtle. Are even the choices we say are ours, not really ours at all?

Theists probably claim that God knows everything, and so he knows the future, including our thoughts before they are formed and our actions before they are performed. Indeed, he knows all about us before we are conceived. This does not necessarily imply, however, that the course of our lives has been decided without us, that we simply go through the pre-ordained motions. God could be a spectator, watching us, through us, as it were;

seeing in advance our fortunes unfold according to what we decide to do and what we are allowed to do.

Moreover, if God did control us, and so we were not personally responsible, God himself would be the instigator of our bad deeds; punishment would be unjust and, considering the miserable existence endured by millions, God would be cruel.

I come to, what seems to me, the most difficult aspect of the matter: it is sometimes proposed that our chemistry dictates our actions – not that our chemicals know our lives in advance, like God, but that they cause our every thought, in every situation. Here we are considering not external, but internal compulsion; and such a notion may appear to be nonsensical. Our chemistry is, of course, part of ourselves, so it remains we who decide.

The same, however, can be said of robots. The robot can decide, but it is doing so according to an internal, prearranged programme. It does not have free will. Similarly, I can choose, but if the choice has, in fact, already been made by the chemicals within me, I do not have free will. I too have been pre-programmed. I am, as it were, a sophisticated robot.

Yet what is the 'me' apart from the physical? I refer to the mind, or, more precisely, to thoughts. On the face of it, I think and conclude and my body acts accordingly. My thoughts control my body, not vice versa.

Chemicals may prompt some thoughts – hunger, for example, proposing the idea of food – but we do not have to obey them; in many cases chemicals do not seem to be involved at all. Suppose I want to write a message and my pen is in another room – I go to the other room to get the pen. My mind makes a simple connection, and my body acts on it. Chemistry may motivate the muscles, but not, it seems clear, the thought.

If what appears to be true is not really true, it is the alternative that needs to be proved.

To show that chemicals cause thoughts one would need to demonstrate that stimulating a chemical causes a certain thought, or that taking away a chemical takes away a certain thought. One would need to be sure that the thought did not arise by any other means – observing, copying and memorising, for example; that it was, indeed, entirely dependent upon the chemical; and this would have to be done for every, single thought. Such a task seems impossibly precise and colossal, and in any case ill-founded, since experience and common sense clearly indicate we are not so dependent upon chemicals.

We are, of course, dependent upon our brains, upon chemical activity, and interference with the brain's functionings, such as a blow on the head, can affect our thoughts, but we do not know what, if any, the thoughts will then be. If it is claimed there is a bond between a specific chemical and a specific thought then, again, it must be shown. Our brains provide the ability to think; they do not seem to tell us what to think. To use a parallel, our eyes enable us to see; they do not dictate what we will see.

These days, there is reference to genes. I understand that scientists can show that certain genes are responsible for certain characteristics. Let us suppose that they could identify every gene, pointing to those which produce mental as well as physical traits. Then by changing the genes they could change the personality. Imagine that scientists pinpointed and removed the gene that produces, say, anger, and so the person affected could not be angry, not even by imitation. Given a situation where one would normally act angrily, how would he react? Quietly? Emotionally? Would he stand firm? Would he walk away? By observing his behaviour we could build up expectations, but we could never be certain what he would think or do – we could suppose, but not know.

We are not just particularly complex machines, for the variables are just too many. We are too open to choice and change, too unpredictable – too personal.

To continue the robot analogy, a robot is pieced together, in every detail, and once assembled it is a finished article. Its purpose is to perform certain, prescribed functions. It is entirely predictable. We may say humans are pieced together in the womb, but once we emerge we are far from finished. We grow and change. We have no obvious purpose, and all that is foreseeable are physical conditions such as we must breathe to live.

As we grow our senses acquaint and accustom us to the world around us, and our minds consider it. Experiences make an impact. Gradually we develop personalities, preferences, perhaps abilities. We emerge as individuals, constantly changing in degree if not fundamentals.

We seem to be a mixture of inherited characteristics, upbringing, interactions in general, likes and dislikes, and personal reflections.

Where chemicals are involved they incline us towards this or that, but they are tempered by other factors, such as experience and knowledge. We judge our response. Thoughts, then, are in command. Mind over matter! Our histories may suggest, perhaps strongly, that we will act in a certain way, but, for a variety of reasons, we may choose otherwise. We may change our minds. We may change our whole way of life. Unless the matter is out of our control, nobody knows what we will do. We think. We decide. We have free will.

Sensations, Ideas and Objects

There is an old conundrum: how do we know a tree exists when nobody is looking at it? The question arises from a line of thought such as, our knowledge of what we call the world around us stems from our senses, from what we see, touch, hear, smell and taste. Our senses give us a sensation of something. This 'something' can be called an idea, but only an idea because we are locked into a world of sense-experience. We cannot go beyond it. Therefore we cannot know that anything exists outside of it. So if nobody is sensing the tree, it may not exist. We don't, and can't know.

This is basically true – we are locked into a world of sense-experience. But there is good reason for thinking that trees, and millions of other things we may rightly call objects, do exist, whether or not they are being observed. Indeed, we may doubt our observations; our senses may be faulty, resulting in us not sensing, but imagining a tree. So it does not exist, even in our senses.

It is confusing to refer to what we are sensing as an idea. Though this may seem appropriate, underlining our dependence upon sense experience, the word 'idea' is commonly used to refer to a thought, particularly a creative or problem-solving thought. Ideas are intangible, internal and personal. Objects, on the other hand, are tangible, they appear external, and can be treated as such, and they are public.

When we sense a tree we can see and touch it, perhaps even smell it – our eyes and fingers, not just our thoughts, provide information about its size, shape, colour and texture. Its image is extremely vivid, precise and unchanging. It is hard and solid. We can make use of it physically, for example, to climb. It seems to be outside of us, and occupying a definite, fixed location. There is no need to explain it to anybody else. They immediately sense what we sense.

We apply reason. Without any prompting others comprehend the tree as we do, in its particulars and as being separate from us. It is likely, therefore, that it does exist independently. How else can it make the same, immediate impact time after time on all normal people?

Solidity itself, which we sense as not being a part of our own body, suggests that whatever we are sensing exists outside of us, and without us, for it is physical, which implies it does not depend on us to be there. It implies it has a structure of its own.

Solids do not just disappear without a physical explanation. Such is our expectation and such is our experience. If a tree is there one day and not the next it is because something has removed it.

Still we are left with the indisputable fact that we are bounded by sense experience, but it would be wrong to conclude that all ideas are of one nature. Our comprehension of a tree received through one or more of the five senses is hugely different to our comprehension of a tree imagined in the mind, so much so that the apparent and reasoned independence and permanency of the first justifies the name object – whereas the second remains literally an idea – and its characteristics give us every confidence in thinking the tree will not vanish if no one is looking at it.

I add as a postscript, does an idea exist when no one is thinking it? Yes, because it is something which has been created and exists until it is completely forgotten. If it is forgotten for a while, and then remembered, it has not ceased to exist. It has been, as it were, asleep. If it is thought of completely anew, it has ceased to exist. It is, as it were, dead.

BEAUTY

The noun 'beauty' can be applied to anything – black eyes, no less! It is perhaps more often expressed as the adjective 'beautiful'. Thus, the weather, scenes, objects, pictures, sounds, tastes, smells, feelings, physical and mental, movements of the limbs, arrangements of words and even moral actions, such as kind or brave ones, can all be described as beautiful.

Given a common morality it may be that moral deeds gain the most consensus as beautiful, though even here disagreement can arise about particular deeds – an apparently kind act can be assessed as really a selfish one, and a brave act as foolish, born of ignorance.

I will concentrate upon beauty as perceived through the five senses, especially through sight, since in my experience the word is most frequently used in speaking of something observed.

Many commentators have linked beauty to pleasure and, indeed, ugliness to displeasure, and this seems to be true enough. It would be masochistic for someone to say they find something beautiful and they dislike it. If the thing belongs to somebody else, they may dislike that, but not the thing itself. To make 'beauty' and 'pleasure' synonymous, however, is too much, for 'beauty' has a certain characteristic, a particular quality of its own. The two words are not interchangeable except in a very colloquial way. Really, beauty causes pleasure. It is not pleasure itself.

So, what is beauty's characteristic or quality? Many words have been proposed: harmony, symmetry, coherence, clarity, gaiety, perfection, significance, expressiveness, usefulness, goodness and universally appreciated. I do not consider any of these prescriptions, or any combinations of them, to be convincing. Something which is beautiful does not have to be useful. We may think all the more of it if it is useful, but seeing it as attractive is what makes it beautiful, irrespective of whether we can do anything with it; nor does beauty have to suggest some truth, or moral, or importance – the subject observed is beautiful because we like the look of it. Gaiety is, by definition, connected with pleasure, and beauty prompts pleasure, but a gay scene may stir no pleasure in a beholder, while a sombre scene may be regarded as most beautiful. One problem with perfection is that we may find a thing beautiful, and then find another thing of the same kind more beautiful which does not mean that we were wrong in the first instance, but that beauty is comparative, and we can never be sure of perfection.

Harmony, symmetry, coherence, clarity are all words that I appreciate. I like patterns, proportions, parts and colours portrayed as in life. So I like representational art, meaning art which reproduces what is actually observed, the kind which some say is pointless since it has been superseded by the camera. Enthusiast or not, we can probably agree that considerable skill is required to produce an accurate likeness and we can all admire the craftsmanship. I am particularly impressed by artists who can paint water and glass. Yet, supposing I saw a picture of, say, a milk bottle, painted ever so accurately, still I don't think I would regard it as beautiful, and no matter how much harmony was contained in an image of a brick wall that too would probably not be beautiful to me, nor a most careful copy of a gruesome scene.

Symmetry does not always amount to beauty, and so say I who favours proportion and balance. My preference is for realism. Another person viewing realistic art may acknowledge the ability of the artist and see some beauty in some works, but consider the form in general to be ordinary, dull and boring. Their idea of beauty is a lack of harmony, wild, innovative imagination, and a clash of colours – fantastic scenarios.

How can anyone say which genre is really beautiful? Examples of either could be accepted as beautiful by some, and by some who are basically on the other side. Two people can look at the same picture, one find it beautiful and the other not, and I don't know any way of deciding one is right and the other wrong. There are no universal criteria, and so we cannot expect universal appreciation.

Considering what we do know, a sensible distinction is drawn between facts and opinions. Certain statements can be tested by immediate and obvious perception, and by definition, and everyone, or nearly everyone, will agree, to the point that anyone who doesn't can be said to be deficient in their senses or understanding. These are factual statements, objective. Opinions draw on values – what is important to us – and judgements – how we balance what is important; and though, of course, values and judgements themselves draw on sense experience and reasoning, they also involve inclinations, influences and an assortment of thoughts, competing with each other and resulting not in one certain answer, accepted by all, but in what seems to us as individuals to be the most satisfactory amalgamation of various factors. Our choice is a personal statement, subjective.

One sort of opinion is commonly known as taste. We like the look, sound, smell, taste or touch of something. We may or may not be able to provide any reason whatsoever. Who can explain why a certain colour is their favourite? Basically, something just appeals to us. It strikes us as attractive. We don't only think it has been well made. We like it. That is the characteristic or quality of beauty, appeal, and different things appeal to different people, a point well recognised by shopkeepers. Think of the multitudes of wallpapers within many, huge pattern books.

Far from universal rules, beauty has no rules at all. As the saying goes, it really is 'in the eye of the beholder' and, I add, also in the ears, nose, mouth and fingers. There is no compelling reason to accept, for example, that Bach's music is more beautiful than Handel's, that roses smell more beautiful than lavender, that fish tastes more beautiful than meat, or that silk feels more beautiful than wool. It is all a matter of personal preference.

Now, as a fact, many of us do like the same things, and sometimes there are underlying features. Humans widely regarded as beautiful are young, neither fat nor thin, with well-defined features and curved figures. Countries display beauty spots, such as expanses of greenery, dotted with woods, lakes and mountains. Not everyone, though, agrees on these characteristics, nor can it be shown that they should, nor might the components add up to beauty even for those who consider them to be prerequisites. We may disagree about particulars, finding this person or that place not beautiful despite it conforming to the usual standards; we may think the correct description is not beautiful, but a word such as distinctive or impressive or remarkable – highlands, for example, are often described as majestic – and we may see beauty in another form in general, such as voluptuous humans and man-made constructions.

Ultimately, however many people consider something to be beautiful, they are not justified in demanding acceptance from others as they would be over a matter of fact. Beauty is not factual. However many common features are detected, they are not binding except for one; that which is beautiful is that which 'strikes a chord' in an individual, and each individual has his own 'chord,' spontaneous, perhaps indescribable, perhaps inexplicable, but there, entirely subjective!

A VERY BRIEF HISTORY OF THE TWENTIETH CENTURY

At the start of the twentieth century there were – as there were throughout preceding centuries – empires. The Western empires formed two alliances which were hostile to each other, and when they clashed in 1914 they ignited a conflict which sucked in so many countries it became known as the First World War. It lasted for four years and killed some ten million people.

Towards the end of the war, in 1917, a revolution broke out in Russia and from it emerged communism, a system which claimed to fortify bodies and certainly impoverished minds. It proclaimed the rule of the proletariat; but just as in England the seventeenth-century revolution, in the name of Parliament, brought forth a dictator, Cromwell; and in France the eighteenth-century revolution, with its uplifting cry of 'liberty, equality, fraternity', resulted in the rule of Napoleon; so in Russia the aim of workers' emancipation produced the tyrant, Joseph Stalin. He decided to modernise his country. His forced industrialisation and collectivisation of agriculture, cost about ten million lives, and his purges to eliminate 'enemies of the people' accounted for millions more. He conducted genocides and built concentration camps.

During the 1920s and '30s much of the world was hit by economic crises. In Germany the Nazi party fed on these, and a general feeling of resentment, to offer a mighty resurgence. It smashed its way to power, and prepared to establish a new, dominant empire. Its leader was another dictator, Adolf Hitler. True to form, he disposed of those he didn't like. He too committed genocide, most notably against the Jews, destroying six million of 'God's chosen people'. Attacking countries that lay around him, he spread Germany's borders ever wider. The expansion was at first tolerated – perhaps the Treaty of Versailles had been too harsh – and then, as his appetite seemed insatiable, it was resisted, so sparking, in 1939, the Second World War. This one lasted six years and killed some thirty-five million people.

After the second, great war a new enmity emerged – between East and West; the East consisting primarily of the Union of Soviet Socialist Republics, mainly Russia, and the neighbours it dominated; the West, of the United States and Western Europe. The rivalry was not only one of power, but also of ideology – capitalism versus communism, democracy versus dictatorship, choice versus compulsion. The USSR closed its borders, drawing across them what was described as 'The Iron Curtain'; it even built a wall through its share of Berlin, to separate it from the West.

What made this 'cold war', as it was called, particularly chilling was that both sides possessed nuclear weapons, weapons so destructive that their explosive power obliterated everything within ten miles, while the lethal dust they unleashed contaminated everything it fell on over hundreds of miles. For the next half a century their missiles, bearing such annihilation, blatantly pointed at each other.

In 1949 China joined the communist camp. Its president, Mao Tse-tung, initially trod the Stalinist path. Later he made his own priorities, but throughout, he, no less than Stalin, shook up his society and brooked no opposition. Again there were concentration camps – indeed there were still over a thousand at the end of the century – and there was genocide, against the Tibetans. The untimely deaths of around forty million to fifty million human beings should lie on Mao Tse-tung's conscience. His emphasis on egalitarianism compelled his citizens – such as survived – to not only think, but even dress the same.

One other particularly appalling overhaul of a country stained Cambodia, in the '70s. Its communist dictator, Pol Pot, cut down over two million of its people, about one quarter of the entire population.

As the richest nation in the world, the USA, faced the largest nation in the world, the USSR, we were told that they possessed enough firepower to wipe out all life on earth, many times over. Perhaps the nearest we came to testing this awful claim was in 1962, over the Cuban missile crisis. The USSR was intent on arming Cuba; the USA on stopping it. The Americans blockaded the island, the Soviets sailed towards it. I remember, as a school-boy, playing rugby the afternoon the two mighty powers approached each other. Now and again we looked at the sky, and called out, with apparent humour, 'I can't see any missiles yet'. Thankfully, we never did; the Soviets turned back.

With the shadow of death hanging over us, we got on with our lives, and in Britain at least, they were not bad lives. The welfare state was born; the standard of living rose. There was more openness, and innovation. One prime minister told us we'd 'never had it so good'. In 1969, men landed on the moon.

The wellbeing of animals and the environment became matters of importance, as did healthy lifestyles, and anti-discrimination in every sphere.

Human beings rather than human robots took over the Kremlin, and its policy softened. The Berlin Wall came down in 1989, and early in the next decade The Soviet Union itself broke down. East and West, though still suspicious, sought rapprochement.

So the century which had given us the biggest wars, the biggest mass murderers, and the very real prospect of total oblivion, ended optimistically. Phew! What next?

THE BIBLE: FACT OR FICTION?

'Is it true?' is a question I was often asked when I taught religious studies. 'There's no proof!' I often heard. Sometimes I would respond with, 'Where is the proof of any ancient history?'

'We have records,' I was told. The Bible is a record, especially of Jewish history.

I recognise, however, that the Bible has accumulated problems. Time after time it mentions God, and we live in an age of increasing disbelief and disinterest in God. It includes stories of miracles, and these days they too are commonly disbelieved. It claims that the world and its life were created in seven days, while evolution has unravelled millions of years. So that's it, God, miracles and accounts of the creation which are largely wrong. In short, more or less, nonsense!

But that is not it! That is very, very far from being it! The two main accounts of the creation are contained in the first two chapters of the first book, Genesis – leaving forty-eight more chapters in Genesis, and sixty-five more books! – yes books! – in the Bible.

As well as the beginning of Genesis, look at Kings. Consider, for example, 2 Kings 17:5–6, 'Then Shalmaneser invaded Israel and besieged Samaria. In the third year of the siege, which was the ninth year of the reign of Hoshea, the Assyrian emperor captured Samaria...' One may quibble about some of the details: probably Shalmaneser died during the assault and the emperor who took the city was Sargon II; also it seems to have fallen in Hoshea's tenth or eleventh year rather than his ninth. But there is no good reason to deny the substance, that the Assyrians attacked and captured Samaria. A layer of carbon found at the site indicates a ferocious fire, so often the fate of conquered cities.

Twenty years later Sargon's son, Sennacherib, attacked Judah. 'In the fourteenth year of the reign of King Hezekiah, Sennacherib, the emperor of Assyria, attacked the fortified cities of Judah and conquered them.' (2 Kings 18:13). His victories were inscribed on clay pillars.

Sennacherib's record of his conquests in Judah

Further archaeological evidence is, for example, the stables, complete with limestone troughs, that King Solomon built for his cavalry at Megiddo. 'Solomon built up a force of … twelve thousand cavalry horses. Some of them he kept in Jerusalem and the rest he stationed in various other cities,' (1 Kings 10:26).

The remains of King Solomon's and, later,
King Ahab's stables at Megiddo

About the year 918, Pharaoh Shishak invaded Israel. 'In the fifth year of Rehoboam's reign King Shishak of Egypt attacked Jerusalem,' (1 Kings 14:25). His own account at Karnak lists his triumphs – not only Jerusalem.

King Ahab's palace, we are told, was 'decorated with ivory' (1 Kings 22: 39), and ivory carvings have been found in the ruins.

The remains of King Ahab's palace

King Hezekiah built a tunnel to ensure a water supply to Jerusalem. 'It was King Hezekiah who blocked the outlet for the Spring of Gihon and channelled the water to flow through a tunnel to a point inside the walls of Jerusalem,' (2 Chronicles 32:30). To this day it is possible to walk through the tunnel.

Hezekiah's tunnel

An inscription in the tunnel describing its construction

In 588 the Babylonians invaded Judah. 'Zedekiah rebelled against King Nebuchadnezzar of Babylonia, so Nebuchadnezzar came with all his army and attacked Jerusalem on the tenth day of the tenth month of the ninth year of Zedekiah's reign.' (2 Kings 25:1). '...The army was also attacking Lachish and Azekah, the only other fortified cities left in Judah' (Jeremiah 34:7). At Lachish correspondence, now known as the Lachish Letters, has been discovered. One letter includes the statement that the lookouts can no longer see the fire signals of Azekah.

Parts of The Lachish Letters

Israelite kings are sometimes mentioned in the histories of other nations; Jehu, for example, whose violent reign is described in 2 Kings 9 and 10. The Babylonians wrote of Jehoiachin. The Bible tells us, 'Jehoiachin was eighteen years old when he became king of Judah...' (2 Kings 24:8).

An Assyrian pillar depicting various scenes.
The second one down shows King Jehu of Israel bowing to King
Shalmaneser of Assyria

The Babylonian Chronicles record the capture of Jerusalem in 597. The Bible states, '...King Jehoiachin ... surrendered to the Babylonians...' (2 Kings 24:12).

Then there is evidence which supports the biblical scene in general. There are quite literally thousands of texts from the Middle East which agree with the way of life outlined in the Bible. The Nuzi texts (fifteenth century BC), for example, describe the custom of a slave becoming an heir, a prospect regretted by Abraham. '...Abram answered "...I have no children ... one of my slaves will inherit my property" ' (Genesis 15:2,3).

Among the towns destroyed by Joshua were Lachish (Joshua 10:31–33), Eglon (Joshua 10:34–35), Debir (Joshua 10:38–39) and Hazor (Joshua 11:10–11), and these places do indeed seem to have fallen in the second half of the thirteenth century, the time when Israel invaded Canaan.

The remains of Hazor

The Philistines repeatedly attacked Israel, as described in 1 Samuel; for example, 1 Samuel 14:52, 'As long as he lived, Saul had to fight fiercely against the Philistines…' Philistine pottery, very distinctive, has been found in and near Jerusalem.

When the kingdom divided into north and south – Israel and Judah – King Asa strengthened Mizpah. '…King Asa gathered men … and ordered them … to fortify the cities of Geba and Mizpah,' (2 Chronicles 16:6). Mizpah's walls have been uncovered. They are twenty feet thick.

These are examples to which many more could be added. Sceptics might like to reflect on the fact that there is almost no archaeological evidence for the battle of Hastings, which occurred not two to three thousand, but roughly one thousand years ago.

How many doubt that Julius Caesar came to Britain in 55 BC? Yet the oldest copy we have of his own account was written about 900 years later. The oldest copies we have of Old Testament books seem to have been written about 100 BC.

In the Gospels, though the story of Jesus feeding, miraculously, 5,000 people may appear incredible, it is more than reasonable to accept that approximately two thousand years ago a person called Jesus preached in Israel. If he didn't, how did Christianity begin?

Consider Luke's emphasis on placing the start of John the Baptist's ministry in history:

> It was the fifteenth year of the rule of the Emperor Tiberius; Pontius Pilate was governor of Judea, Herod was ruler of Galilee, and his brother Philip was ruler of the territory of Iturea and Trachonitis; Lysanias was ruler of Abilene, and Annas and Caiaphas were high priests...

Luke 3:1–2

A stone slab, found at Caesarea, with the names Tiberius and Pontius Pilate inscribed on it

Josephus was a Jewish historian of the first century. The copy we have of his *The Antiquities of the Jews* includes the following:

> At about this time lived Jesus, a wise man, if indeed one might call him a man. For he was one who accomplished surprising feats and was a teacher of such people as are eager for novelties. He won over many of the Jews and many of the Greeks. He was

the Messiah. When Pilate, upon an indictment brought by the principal men among us, condemned him to the cross, those who had loved him from the very first did not cease to be attached to him. On the third day he appeared to them restored to life, for the holy prophets had foretold this and myriads of other marvels concerning him. And the tribe of the Christians, so called after him, has to this day still not disappeared.

Judging from Josephus' writings in general it seems that he was not a Christian, which makes some statements in the passage very suspicious – perhaps they are additions by believers – while other statements, such as the last sentence, support the overall conclusion that, indeed, he was not a Christian. Later, Josephus refers to Jesus as 'called the Christ'. But from this apparent non-believer there is affirmation that Jesus at least lived and died as the Gospels describe.

Another historian, certainly not a Christian, who mentions the religion and its founder was the Roman, Tacitus, writing in the first twenty years of the second century. He states that following the great fire in Rome in AD 64 Emperor Nero:

...fabricated scapegoats – and punished with every refinement the notoriously depraved Christians (as they were popularly called). Their originator, Christ, had been executed in Tiberius' reign by the governor of Judaea, Pontius Pilate. But in spite of this temporary setback the deadly superstition had broken out afresh, not only in Judaea (where the mischief had started), but even in Rome.

The Bible, then, is not just about myths and miracles. It is not without extra-biblical evidence. Certainly, if you read a work claiming to be factual and you are doubtful about some of the so-called facts, you wonder about all of them, but it would be illogical to reject all of them. You consider each as it comes. Does it seem plausible? Is there anything to support it? If not, is there any sound reason to deny it? Does it fit the context in general?

So far as the Bible is concerned, sceptics do not usually doubt that the Babylonians invaded Jerusalem – once the event has been pointed out to them – but that God parted the Red Sea. What they shrink from is the supernatural. Although I have not classified each sentence, I think it probable that most statements in the Bible are of the straightforward, not supernatural, kind. Therefore, to risibly dismiss sixty-six mostly historical books as nonsense because a minority of parts of them are unacceptable is itself nonsensical.

Where God and miracles are mentioned, they can be seen as matters of interpretation, according to faith. To see them as lies is harsh, and very probably wrong. The writers and their subjects were not trying to persuade people to believe in God and his power. Both were accepted already. If God wanted something to happen, he made it happen. Holy men, through the power of God, performed miracles.

What persuaded Jesus' own disciples to become Christians? A miracle! The Gospels suggest, as does reasonableness, that following the crucifixion the disciples were disillusioned, dispirited and frightened. Soon they were full of spirit, sure that Jesus had been brought back to life, so sure that they proclaimed their belief even if it brought about their own deaths. Hardly the action of men who knew that really they were telling lies!

Whatever we ourselves make of the resurrection, of every miracle, of every reference to God, there remains too much of the Bible for it to be cast contemptuously aside. If we do not believe in God, it does not follow that we should not believe in King David. If we do not accept that Jesus walked on water, we do not also have to accept that Jesus never existed. Did Mohammed never exist because there is a tradition that he ascended to heaven on a white horse?

Returning to the battle of Hastings, I cite an extract from *The Anglo-Saxon Chronicle*, probably written not long after the event:

> King Harold was slain, and Leofwine, his brother, and earl Gurth, his brother, and many good men. The French had possession of the place of slaughter, as God granted them because of the nation's sins.

Another extract, this one from Bede's *A History of the English Church and People*, written in the eighth century and referring to Oswald, king of Northumbria, who died in 642:

> Oswald's great devotion and faith in God was made evident by the miracles that took place after his death. For at the place where he was killed fighting for his country against the heathen, sick men and beasts are healed to this day.

Are we to say that Oswald never lived because of his association with miracles, or that the battle of Hastings never happened because the writer claims God allowed the French to win as a punishment? More likely, we will assent to the straightforward and recognise that the supernatural was more apparent to past ages than to the present one.

Consider, also, the moral teaching contained in the Bible. '...an eye for an eye...' (Deuteronomy 19:21) is the basis of justice. Every country in the world prohibits murder and theft, both prohibited by the ten commandments. Can you think of a better moral standard for society than Jesus' 'Do for others what you want them to do for you...' (Matthew 7:12)?

The plain truth is, many people who dismiss the Bible have scarcely ever, if at all, opened it; their knowledge is limited to a vague, skimpy summary of a few scattered stories, almost entirely miracles; their reaction is prompted by cultural pressure in general and peer pressure in particular. The Bible is not just a prop for weak-minded goody-goodies. Read it for what it is – a huge collection of facts, beliefs and literature.

What is my own answer to the question, is the Bible true? Historically? In general, yes. Theologically? I don't know, but my own inclination is that God probably does not exist. Morally? I cannot improve on the idea of treating others as we would like to be treated. Supernaturally? Again, I don't know, but again I think miracles probably do not happen. So, I conclude, a mixture, true and untrue!

AN ATHEIST'S VIEW OF JESUS CHRIST

There is no sound reason for denying that Jesus ever lived. The Jewish and Roman setting is authentic. Figures such as the Roman emperors Augustus and Tiberius, the governor, Pontius Pilate, King Herod and the high priests, Annas and Caiaphas, can be clearly pinpointed in fact. Jesus' own life is summarised by the historian, Josephus, writing in the first century, and details are also given by the historian, Tacitus, writing in the first twenty years of the second century.

Before us is the story of an individual who lived in Israel about two thousand years ago. He became a religious and moral teacher, but his teachings so upset the authorities that they executed him. All quite believable; there have been many other such martyrs.

I do not accept a miraculous birth, nor resurrection. Indeed, I reject virtually all of the miracles, but I say 'virtually' because there are strange cases – and recent ones – of some sick people being healed without any medical explanation. The Roman Catholic Church investigates thoroughly a professed miracle before declaring it really is one. 'The devil's advocate' strives to find a scientific solution. Consider the psychosomatic argument: that sometimes the power of a person's mind, perhaps in conjunction with another, can reduce, if not end, an illness. It may be there were times when Jesus' charisma, coupled with a sufferer's expectations, triggered such a process.

Moreover, though the miracle itself may not have happened, some of the account could be true. For example, in the 'feeding of the 5,000' Jesus could, as described, have been speaking to a large crowd who grew hungry. Perhaps he shared what food he possessed, and this prompted many to share their food so that everyone had enough to eat. Other so-called miracles may have grown up from a real occasion.

Then, as now, there is the influence of exaggeration and rumour. Around a well-known personality, tales can abound. In a religious age, when wondrous events were broadly accepted, it is not surprising that some were attached to a prophet. Many more are narrated in gospels which the church did not include in its bible. These miracles were probably not outright lies – there was no need for them to be. People believed already.

Whatever actually happened, the disciples became convinced of the resurrection of Jesus. They truly believed he rose from the dead, for it defies sense to claim that they set out, determined to proclaim the Gospel, expecting it to bring about their own gruesome deaths, while knowing that really they were telling lies. Theirs was the spirit expressed so resoundingly and absolutely by Paul: '…I am certain that nothing can separate us from his (Christ's) love: neither death nor life, neither angels nor other heavenly rulers or powers, neither the present nor the future, neither the world above nor the world below-there is nothing in all creation that will ever be able to separate us from the love of God which is ours through Christ Jesus our Lord,' (Romans 8:38–39).

Jesus implied that he had not come to change the law, but to expound it. He said the most important commandment was, 'Love the Lord your God…' (Mark 12:30) and the second most important was, '…Love your neighbour as you love your-self…'(Mark 12:31). Both commands come from the Old Testament. He did, however, give his own version of what has become known as mankind's golden rule, 'Do for others what you want them to do for you…'(Matthew 7:12).

It is unnatural, though not unknown, for people to love others as much as they love themselves, or to put others first because they would like others to put them first; but we can be courteous, considerate and helpful to those who are around us just as we would like them to be courteous, considerate and helpful to us. All very practical, attainable, pleasurable and beneficial, creating a better, happier society.

As the victim, in the parable of 'The Good Samaritan', lay injured, no doubt he longed for someone to help him. So would we. The Samaritan did help, and if we acted similarly we would be applying our natural feeling of compassion, drawing satisfaction from our assistance, and gaining the goodwill and respect of the victim and of everyone else who became involved in the affair.

Of course, it is not every day that we find someone hurt on the roadside, but there are many days when we can provide some small assistance, such as returning to someone an object they have dropped, showing a stranger the way or slowing to allow a car to emerge from a side road onto a main road. Such actions make life more pleasant all-round.

We are told that Jesus healed the sick, and to some extent he was concerned about the poor. Helping the needy! We can only guess how many benevolent deeds have been performed over the ages because the helpers have done what they believed Jesus wanted them to do. Charities, hospitals and schools have been established because of their founder's Christian beliefs. The religion has brought much good, and to those who retort it has brought much harm, I say it is not the teaching – love enemies, turn the other cheek – that has caused wars, but some men's intolerance of other men's interpretations.

Jesus also implied that he had come to fulfil the words of the prophets. A major prophetic theme was that a great king would end the sufferings of an oppressed people. He would rule in glory and they would live in happiness. This king was known as the Messiah or the Christ. The New Testament tells us that Jesus saw himself as the Christ; the title has become his surname, and his followers known as Christians.

The plan presented is that though Jesus was well aware of his unique status, he spent his earthly years as a wandering preacher. He foresaw that his words would cause his death, and he died as a sacrifice, so that believers might be saved. He anticipated being restored to life and ascending into heaven. One day, probably while some of his contemporaries were still alive, he would return as the Christ, gather the righteous, destroy the evil, and establish the everlasting kingdom of God.

It can always be claimed that the facts have been overlaid by the message: that certainly Jesus antagonised the authorities, but that his arrest and execution were unexpected and unavoidable. However, I know of no evidence that his end came against his will. The Gospels suggest that he could have saved his life even as he stood before his final judge on earth, Pontius Pilate.

Whatever the case, I admire him, firstly for having the strength of character to turn away from a conventional lifestyle. The attractions of family, home, comfort and security are almost overwhelming, and they absorb most of us. Anyone who deliberately gives them up is making a great sacrifice. Jesus chose to commit himself to his teaching. He was prepared to live in poverty.

He said what he believed, deferring to no one. His words are definite, and many of his sentences are majestic. 'The people ... were amazed at the way he taught ... he taught with authority,' (Mark 1:22). He was perceptive, his responses were quick and they could be withering. He escaped the Pharisees' trap about paying taxes (Mark 12:13–17), told the Sadducees that their carefully constructed dilemma about the resurrection was irrelevant, and their denial of life after death wrong (Mark 12:18–27), and after he had dealt with the question of the most important commandment (Mark 12:28–34), it is stated that 'nobody dared' to ask him 'any more questions' (Mark 12:34). His parables reveal a most fertile imagination. Even without the miracles, Jesus was a very impressive person.

Suppose he did go to his death reluctantly but willingly. The bravery required is simply astounding. He knew that he would be nailed, hands and feet, to a cross, exposed to the elements, insects, taunts and petty acts of cruelty; and there he would stay pinned, for hours, perhaps days, in agony, slowly deteriorating until eventually he died. No wonder Pilate marvelled at his silence and pointed out, '...I have the authority to set you free and also to have you crucified,' (John 19:10).

So Jesus died, and, to my mind, he remains dead. But, what a legacy! He has raised morality to the height of perfection, given hope to millions, maybe billions, and inspired more acts of kindness, great and small, than will ever be known. In terms of the number of believers, and lives significantly touched by his own, Jesus Christ is by far the most influential person who has ever lived.

THE SERMON,
OR ONE REASON – ALBEIT THE WRONG
ONE – FOR READING THE BIBLE

The preacher mounted the pulpit, laid out his wares, flashed his surplice, eyed up the congregation, and ejaculated:

'Brethren, the Christian message is bare for all to behold. Yet there are parts which, at first peering, seem somewhat queer. I would be shrinking from the prick, betraying my manhood, if I did not uncover the fact, one might say, the facts, of life, and it is one such part I desire to pull out now in an unashamedly full-frontal exposure.

'My text is the Gospel of St Luke, chapter 17, verse 34, "I tell you, in that night there shall be two men in one bed; the one shall be taken, and the other shall be left."

'The setting is the Day of Judgement. Jesus is telling us that come that great event, one man will be saved and the other perish. Clear enough! The problem rises up with "…in that night there shall be two men in one bed…" We blush, we recoil, but the issue forces its point into us. What, we gasp, are two men doing in one bed?

'I fear it is a sign of the times that at once lewdness stirs and swells. Out with it! Are the men, to use a word which once meant simply "happy", gay? If so, they are committing a grave sin! Be in no doubt about the thrust of that truth. Leviticus commands, "Thou shalt not lie with mankind, as with womankind: it is abomination". And forget not what befell the men of Sodom who desired to know, a biblical euphemism, the strangers in their midst. They were blinded and burned!

'Today we are expected to embrace homosexuality. We live, as did Lot and his wife, affronted by an anything goes, one might say, "anything comes, off", morality. There is even the creeping movement, shame it is to say, of sodomites donning the clerical frock. Imagine! Pity the choirboys! Pity the choir – always on a treble note!

'In a sense – not a physical one – men can love one another. David loved Jonathan, but he extolled Jonathan's love for him as surpassing that of women. It penetrated beyond the externals and into the heart. David's amorous predilections protruded at the sight of the naked, and aptly named, Bathsheba. Remember, late one afternoon David was strolling upon his palace roof when he spotted an exquisitely beautiful woman bathing. Picture the scene! Perhaps, as "The Song of Solomon" has it – and with seven hundred wives and three hundred mistresses Solomon ought to know – Bathsheba's breasts were like twin deer feeding among lilies, like bunches of grapes, and the curve of her thighs like the work of an artist. Solomon compares his beloved to a palm tree and is intent on climbing it and picking its fruit. Well, what Solomon intended, David did; not that he forced his temptress, oh no! It seems that she was willing enough. Again, to pluck from "The Song of Solomon", she might have succumbed with, "I have already undressed; why should I get dressed again?" and, "I am trembling; you have made me as eager for love as a chariot driver is for battle". No doubt she panted at the sight of what was presented to her. And so the two became one.

'As surely as night follows day, however, punishment follows lust, and one punishment was that David's own mistresses were defiled by his own son, deliberately, in full, public gaze, on the palace roof, under a tent, no doubt a very thin one, erected according to purpose. And we think we invented uncensored sex! You might imagine that after such a deflating experience David turned his back on women for evermore, but no! Even on, or rather, in his deathbed he was kept warm by a most attractive girl, again rather appropriately named, Abishag, though, we are assured, the connection did not extend that far, probably because of David's old age. Women instead of hot-water bottles, an interesting treatment not yet available, I believe, on the NHS!

'So we see the power of the weaker sex. A woman by her beauty, accentuated by make-up – remember Jezebel and Esther – can so easily lead a man astray. A wink, a wiggle, a thrust and the

spell is at work! That masterpiece, once more, "The Song of
Solomon" compares a woman exciting men to a mare exciting
stallions. Her lover is like an apple tree and its fruit is sweet to her
taste. Their love must not be interrupted. Should a man, by some
mighty feat of will, resist the charms, a woman scorned can
indeed flick a hellish whip. Potiphar's wife beseeched Joseph to
"come to bed" and when he refused, she clung onto his robe,
claimed rape and had him imprisoned. Beware, young sirs!

'I suppose the man who winced most under the clutches of
women was Samson. His wife betrayed his riddle, his enemies
gathered while he still lay with a woman of easy virtue, and, with
floods of tears, the female's weapon in disguise, Delilah drew
from him the secret of his manhood. Soon he could no longer
gaze upon that which had so pleased him.

'Such guile in comely form! Rahab the prostitute cunningly
concealed her customers from their enemies, Tamar played the
prostitute and became pregnant by her own father-in-law, Judah;
while the daughters of Lot, bemoaning that there was not a man
to come into them, even turned their cravings upon their own
father, intoxicated him and committed incest with him while he
was insensible of the experience. No wonder Ecclesiastes found
that a woman was more bitter than death, that Zechariah chose a
woman to represent wickedness and that John, author of the book
of Revelation, portrayed obscenity as the great harlot.

'It was harlots that made the prodigal son prodigal. The book
of Proverbs paints a graphic picture of their shenanigans: they lie
in wait, on street corners, in the darkness, and as a young man
passes by, one seizes him and kisses him. "Come," she entices,
"my couch is covered with fine, perfumed linen. Come, let us
swell each other with love." And they do just that, becoming, as
Paul noted, "all puffed up". The man imagines he is entering
heaven, but really he is being sucked into hell. To return to
Proverbs, "Don't be tempted by their beauty; don't be trapped by
their flirting eyes." If you go into them, "you are travelling the
road to death".

'Oh, wicked sirens! Jeremiah exposes them, "You are like a
wild camel on heat, running about loose ... when she is on heat,
who can control her? No male that wants her has to trouble

himself; she is always available at mating time." Ezekiel looked forward to the day when she would be stripped and left completely naked in front of everyone, gathered around her in a circle. Similarly, Hosea threatened his wayward wife: nymphomaniacs will be stripped as naked as the day they were born, fenced in with thorn bushes, blocked by a wall. Like the women of Samaria, damned by Amos, they will be impaled on hooks. They will twist and groan, as Micah enthuses, like a woman giving birth. Bared and shamed, they will be covered in filth, observed Nahum, and so they should be for they have wallowed in filth. May they, in the vivid words of the second book of Kings, "eat their excrement and drink their urine".

'Not to our taste, I know, but the prophets did not mince their words, nor be partial when they dished out their justice, whatever its substance. Let us, like them, show no sexual favours. We too will be asexual. As we have seen, men as well as women can do a bit of wallowing. Oh yes, it takes two to tango, in Paris or anywhere else. And so I turn to the backside. Ezekiel appreciated that women can be "filled with lust", but "lust for oversexed men with large sex organs". The men are the stallions to the mares, "well-fed stallions, wild with desire, each lusting for his neighbour's wife," warns Jeremiah. Some sons, Ezekiel saw, sleep – an impossible euphemism – with their father's wife, while Amos spotted sons and fathers up to the hilt with the same slave-girl; he does not make clear whether or not at the same time. Some men, Ezekiel adds, force women to endure intercourse with them during their period and, I myself add, some force women to receive the rub in or out of their period. Yes, I cry, rape!

'Amnon cunningly pretended he was ill and when his half-sister, no less, came to his bedside he dragged her in and had his wicked way. Rape was the lot of women when a besieged city fell, as Zechariah foretold vigorously for Jerusalem; the book of Lamentations lays bare wives and daughters "forced to submit". When the tribe of Benjamin was in danger of dying out, the men simply captured virgins from the towns around and compelled them to be their wives. No wonder the book of Judges ends with the words, "Everyone did just as he pleased." Real freedom! We can but imagine – and should try to – the degradations thrust

upon, and indeed into, the concubine, also unclothed in the book
of Judges, who was shut out of the house and used in every
conceivable way, throughout the night, as a sexual toy – the type
described in some of the more lurid catalogues I receive from
time to time. The penalty for rape was death. Poor Haman was
hanged because his pleas for mercy were mistaken as an attempted
violation of the queen. But there was a way out: if the woman was
not already married or engaged, the rapist must marry her. What a
way of procuring the wife of your dreams! A truly happy ending!

'Marriage, though, was not the ideal. Paul teaches that it
would be better for a man not to marry, but it prevents forni-
cation, and did not God create Eve as a companion for man? They
became one body. A wife, the book of Proverbs decides, is a good
thing, though not a nagging wife. To continue with Paul, the
husband is supreme, the wife reflects his glory, learning in silence,
submitting to him. She does not control her own body, her
husband does – an injunction I have inscribed above my bed. A
wife is to please her husband. Starting as a virgin, likened by
Isaiah to a city unconquered, she opens her gates, her husband
enters and she becomes, in the simile of the psalmist, like a
fruitful vine. Entwined, they should not stray. To remould
Isaiah's stipulation, the only naked couple to climb into their large
bed should be them.

' "No adultery" is the seventh commandment. According to
the Old Testament, if a husband suspected his wife of unfaithful-
ness he could take her to the priest, who would give her water
mixed with earth to drink – unpleasant, but, if innocent,
harmless; if guilty, her sexual zones would shrivel, and her
stomach swell. Enough to bring tears to any eyes! The man, for
his part, should 'possess his vessel,' in Paul's discreet words, and
employ it properly. Remember Onan: because he withdrew,
repeatedly, at the point of climax, from his brother's widow, and
so she did not conceive, God killed him. If, Job concedes, he
longs for another man's wife then may his own wife lie down in
another man's bed, to which I add may she not, like the woman
mentioned by Ezekiel, become "worn out".

'Our Lord, aiming as always for perfection, pronounced that
lust itself is tantamount to adultery, and bids us cut off any part of

our body that causes us to sin; in this context, another eye-watering solution. Paul called upon us to "mortify our members". Again I reach for a handkerchief. Yet when Jesus was confronted by the woman caught in adultery he responded with forgiveness. Who is without sin? Christianity tempers command with charity, and even the Old Testament, prepared to burn and stone, drew back from cutting off – though not into – the male protuberance. Was not the sign of the covenant circumcision? A man who, by some misfortune, was without his organ was not allowed to participate in worship. Should a woman grab a man by "the secrets", even to save her husband, it was her hand that was cut off. The secrets were supreme. I wonder if Paul was thinking of them when in describing the parts of the body he reminded us, with fond memories, that we give greater honour to the inferior.

'Heaven forbid, though, that we should misuse the inferior, and so I return to my text and my question, why are two men in one bed? We read of a man in bed with his children; that can be explained as protection. But two men in bed with each other opens one, or even two, black holes, except, notice, one man will be saved and the other damned. To be saved he must be innocent. Therefore he is being forced by the other. I can scarcely bring myself to utter the words, but strain and push I will – male rape! Oh, abomination of desolation! Brethren, have I not given you examples enough? Can you not picture the scene? Beat down the desires, sit upon the unnatural acts and, indeed, tie down the natural ones, no matter what the ecstasy. Hold before you always the solemn words of the book of Proverbs, that you should not expend all your energy on, *sex*!'

Inflamed by righteous indignation at the things he had roused, the preacher swept up his books; the force of his movement knocked one to the floor. 'Bugger!' he was heard to mutter, as he bent down to retrieve it, quickly followed by, 'Eeee!'

Printed in the United Kingdom
by Lightning Source UK Ltd.
134028UK00001B/193/P

9 781847 483034